Quinlan

FOSTER'S PRIDE BOOK 3

KATHI S. BARTON

World Castle Publishing, LLC
Pensacola, Florida
Copyright © Kathi S. Barton 2021
Paperback ISBN: 9781955086202
eBook ISBN: 9781955086219
First Edition World Castle Publishing, LLC, May 10, 2021
http://www.worldcastlepublishing.com
Licensing Notes
Cover: Karen Fuller
Editor: Maxine Bringenberg

Prologue

Glancing at the clock, Lily counted down the time she had left to work. Her feet hurt, her back was killing her, and she thought if she were to sit down right now, she'd never get up again. This was the problem with being overeducated, unmarried, with four kids at home wondering where their next meal was coming from. Smiling, she thought of her sister and what she was going to say to her when she arrived tomorrow night.

Lily knew the first thing she was going to say to her. She'd want to know where the hell her head had been when she'd taken on three kids that weren't hers. Lily would tell her what she said to anyone that asked. She loved them.

But she also knew Rogue would love them too. If nothing else, her sister would strive to be the best aunt to them and would love them as much as she did. Her sister was one of a kind.

A year and a half ago, Lily had been happy, about to be married and living in a home for the first time in her adult life. Then, as life would sometimes do, it shit on her. Mark was killed in a robbery. She assumed, sadly so, that she and the kids would be taken care of. But that didn't pan out either.

His ex-wife had sued her for the house and insurance before Mark had even been buried. Not only did she win the suit against her—even though everything, from the insurance and house to the cars in the garage, were in her name with Mark's—in the end, Lily had been left with nothing. Less than nothing because while she'd been earning a nice check each week, the money had been in the checking account she'd shared with Mark. The bitch had gotten her money too.

The kids, however, had been nothing Missy, his ex-wife, had wanted. They were hers, of course, but since Mark had won full custody of them, she saw no reason to take them with her when she robbed them of even a home to live in. The attorney for Missy had told Lily several times how sorry he was and that he wished he'd been on her side. Lily was glad she was there for them when their father had loved them so dearly. Even her own son, Gabe, Mark had treated the same as he had his own children.

"Lily, there's a phone call for you. I think it's

your daughter." Nodding, she took the call in the boss's office of the restaurant she worked in. Billy, at fifteen, was in charge of the others when she had to work.

"Mom, there is a person here who says she's your sister. She's nothing like you, is she? If she is your sister. I don't know if I like her or not." Lily laughed and asked her to put her on the phone. "I'd have to let her in. Are you willing to bet she's your sister?"

"All right. To test your theory, and it is a good one, ask her what her first name is. If she won't tell you, it's her. By the way, her middle name is Rogue. She won't allow anyone to call her by her first one." She heard Billy asking her what her first name was and the reply she got from Rogue.

"You tell your mother that I'm going to kick her ass all the way to my car and back if she so much as gives anyone my fucking first initial. You tell her I didn't come all this way to—" Billy must have believed her because she was talking to Rogue as she finished talking about the things she was going to do to her when she found her. "I'm not above kicking your ass, even though you're older than me."

"I believe you. I'm so glad you're there. But I thought you weren't coming until tomorrow. What happened?" Rogue didn't answer her but asked a question of her own. "Yes, we're staying in a one-bedroom apartment. It's all I can afford. There is plenty of room if you discount the fact that I'm rarely home anymore, trying to keep up with the rent and food for the five of us."

"One of them is giving me the evil eye right now. Doesn't she know I'm her aunt and the one she should be buttering up?" Lily told Rogue they didn't understand buttering people up, as they didn't know anyone with anything they would share with them. "You need to get you a good attorney, Lily. If I had been around, she never would have gotten away with this."

"Yes, well, that costs money. Money I don't have. I'm so glad you're here. I've missed you. Where are you going to stay?" She asked her if she could move them in with her. "I don't know, Rogue. Are you still living out of a suitcase?"

"Pretty much. But today I'm in a hotel that has three rooms and a kitchenette. I'm going to gather the kids up, hit a pizza place, and meet you after work." She told her the name of the hotel she was staying at. "If you want, I can come pick you up. The kid in charge here said you walked to work because you have no car. Didn't I tell you I'd pay for one for you to use until I could make it back here?"

"That would be Billy. She's fifteen." Rogue asked her how she could keep them all straight. "You can do that when you love them as much as I do. I'll be getting off here at around eleven. If you could pick me up, I'd love it. I'm too exhausted to walk much more today."

Lily knew that by the time she got home, not only would Rogue have all their names straight, but she'd know everything there was to know about them. She'd even bet they'd have a few changes of good clothing, a toy or two if they wanted, and Billy and Gabe, the oldest two, would have some kind of handheld game that Rogue knew how to play as well as any teenager.

At eleven, Lily clocked out. She'd done well in tips tonight and was still counting them out when her sister pulled up in a gray SUV. All four of her children were in the back seats and buckled in properly. Lily asked her what she was doing with such a big car.

"I rented it while I'm here. By the way, I was told none of them needed to be in a car seat. I'm still thinking smart mouth back there, Donna, needs to have a roll of tape over her mouth. She's just like me." With a large grin from Rogue, Lily turned to look at Donna. She gave her a thumbs up. "I'm moving you into a house I rented. I don't want to hear about how you're fine in that place you were at. There is only one bathroom and five people sharing it. You know me, can't stand to share anything."

"You're a wonderful sharer. Is that a word?"

Rogue pulled out of the parking lot and onto the road. It was on the tip of her tongue to ask her how far she was going to be walking now but she didn't. The kids were talking quietly, the music, something that Rogue had on all the time, was just background noise, and the seat was comfy.

Being awakened by the door opening and the light coming on startled her. Turning in the seat to count the kids, something she did every time they were out, she saw they were pulling things from the back of the car. Getting out, Rogue handed her a heavy bag of what appeared to be food and told her to take it into the house.

It was just after one in the morning when the kids finally made it up to the bedrooms. Lily just wanted to lie down and never wake up, but Rogue said she wanted to talk to her about something. Lily had seen how much she'd paid for the food before Rogue had snatched the receipt from her and wanted to say a few things to her as well.

"Okay. Two things. I can afford whatever is running through your mind to say to me about the purchases tonight. More if you need it. The house belongs to a buddy of mine who is out of the country right now. In effect, we're doing him a favor, he told me, by being here and keeping the lights on. Also, I have another friend that has a brother who is an attorney. I'm going to call him first thing in the morning. There is no reason whatsoever she should have gotten anything at all from Mark's estate." Lily felt her eyes fill with tears. "If you start crying, I'm going to cry, and we're going to be a slobbery mess when the kids get up in a few hours."

"I've so missed you." They hugged again. They'd been hugging since they got here, and it felt better every time they did. "Missy, the kids' mom, told the judge right there in the courtroom that the kids were heathens anyway and should be with me. Rogue, the kids were in the room when she said that. How could anyone do that to a child, let alone their own child?"

"There are plenty of people out there that would, and who do it daily. She's shit, and we're going to take care of her as soon as possible." Lily told her she hoped so. "I know you've not done it yet, so I will. We need to call Dad and make him aware of what is going on. I know you and him parted on bad terms, but this isn't likely to get resolved soon, and it would be nice if he was in your corner."

"He was having an affair when Mom was laying there dying." Rogue didn't comment, but she knew what she was thinking. "It doesn't matter that Mom had been in a coma for eight years. He should have been faithful to her. Getting married not a month after she was laid to rest was a terrible thing to do to her memory."

"What sort of memories do you have of Mom, Lily? Want me to tell you about mine? She had a stroke when I was barely two. From that point on, the only time I saw her was when Dad would load us up in the car and take us to see her at the nursing home. I haven't any idea what her voice sounded like. I don't know the color of her eyes. She wasn't ever able to do any of the things for me that she did for you when you were younger. No cookie baking. No PTA meetings. Mom was in a coma when I needed her. How do you think Dad coped when he needed someone?" Lily told her it wasn't Mom's fault. "No, it wasn't anyone's fault. Mom had a stroke that took her away from both of us, but especially Dad. And he did try. You know that."

"I know. But only a month. I was just getting used to not going to see her when he married again." Rogue again said nothing. "I guess we're still going to agree to disagree about this."

"I suppose so. But I have something I'd like for you to think about. We had each other when Mom was alive. Dad had no one. Did he ever bring her to our home? Did Dad ever once mention to either of us that he was finding love someplace else? No, he didn't. You want to know why he might have done that? Because he never wanted us to be hurt. I think what he did in sparing us was more loving than anything anyone could have done for us." Lily hadn't thought of it that way. "Another thing he did too. He didn't ever not visit Mom every day. He took care of her the best he could when she came home from the nursing home in those last days. He did this, all by himself, while we got to live and have a life. Dad did all of that for us. Then after Mom passed, Dad got to live for himself. I think what he did took a great deal of courage. Things could have been a great deal different if he'd not loved and respected Mom the way he did."

When Rogue went to bed, Lily sat there for another hour. Everything Rogue said was true. Some of it was things she'd said to her before, but thinking back on the way they had lived while their mom was alive, Lily could see their dad trying hard to make their lives as normal as possible. Yes, he'd done that, and more, for both of them. Lily decided to give him a call tomorrow.

Lily got up at seven, nearly an hour after she should have been up and moving. The kids were going to be late for school. They didn't have their lunches made, and she was really thinking about letting them stay home for the day when she made it to the kitchen. The house was empty of any sound. The note on the table had her snatching it up, sure that someone had taken her children from her.

"Breathe and calm the hell down." She let out a long breath when she read the first words that her sister had written on the note. "I gave the kids lunch money and took them to school. Gabe has given me a list of things they'll need now, and I'm picking it up on the way home. If you're reading this, just sit down, calm down, and have whatever you drink in the morning, and I'll be there soon. Christ, I love these kids."

Lily was brewing a cup of tea that was on the counter when Rogue came back. Her usual brew was a cup of coffee, but there didn't seem to be a coffee maker in the room. Helping her bring in the things she'd picked up, Lily was positive that a computer wasn't on the list her son had given his aunt.

"It wasn't. I need it. If they can use it too, that's fine by me. But I have several shots I need to take care of and get them printed. Your boss called this morning. He said the place has been closed up for the next ten days. Something about a fire inspector. Are you really working at a place that needs to be shut down by the fire marshal?" Lily told her sister what had happened last night. "Okay, having the fire extinguisher go off over the stove is messy. It'll be more than ten days, I'm betting. They'll have to inspect it before he'll be able to reopen. If they find any of that retardant on anything in the kitchen area, he'll shut you down again."

Lily didn't care how messy it was to clean up. All she could focus on was not having money coming in for ten days or more. Rogue shook her shoulders. She must have said something to her several times.

There was a look of complete concern on her face just then.

"Are you going to listen to me now?" Nodding, she said she would. "Good. As I've told you several times, I have enough money to support you and the kids until we get this court thing looked into. If you can hold the fort down while I make a few calls, maybe I can get it resolved before the restaurant reopens, and you won't have to go back. Just chill out. Together we can keep the kids happy and fed. Don't freak out about money, Lily. I told you, I make great money at my job, and I don't have anyone or anything to spend it on but you and the kids. All right? Say it's all right, Lily."

"It's all right." Hugging her sister, something that she was coming to depend on to get her going, she looked at her when they were apart. "I'm also going to call Dad. You're right. I was being selfish to him."

"I never said that." Lily said she knew that too but felt that way. "I have his number. I'll give it to you. Then I'm going to call my buddy. If he can't help us, I'm betting he knows someone that can."

Lily got the number and wondered at the area code. It occurred to her that she had no idea where her dad was living nor what he was doing with his life. Picking up the phone to call him, she decided that she needed to get help. There wasn't anything she could do alone that wouldn't go much better with help.

Lexi answered the phone on the second ring.

"Hello, Lexi. It's Lily. Is there any way I can talk to my dad for a little bit?" Lexi said he'd just gone to the store, but she'd love to talk to her. "I've a major problem here...."

Telling her everything she had going on, Lily and Lexi were both sobbing by the time her dad was back home and available to talk to her. She wanted her daddy here. After promising Lexi a hug, Lily wanted a hug from her dad too.

Chapter 1

"This looks good, don't you think? I mean, we'll need some of those fancy crackers to go with it too." Her sister growled at her. "Now what? Lily, you told me the kids like cheese." She put the three-pound roll of cheese in her cart, only to have her sister take it out again. "Am I going to have to go behind you again to let the kids pay for it? You said it will make a great after-school snack. I'm helping with that."

"Right now, you have—let me count—six three-pound rolls of different kinds of cheese in this cart. Even if they were to have cheese every day after school until they graduate, there isn't any way they'll be able to eat all this. Not to mention, I wonder for their digestive systems too."

"She means we might not be able to poop, Aunt Rogue." Rogue winked at Donna when she walked by her, picking up the roll of cheese and putting it back in the cart. "I would love some beef jerky too, but I think it would be cheaper for us to buy the cow. What do you think?"

Both she and her sister laughed at Donna. Then Lily looked at her with the face she used on the kids. She was upset. Not mad, but upset. Rogue knew why, but she didn't want to have to tell her once again that she could afford it.

"Don't. Okay? Just don't tell me again how much this is costing me. Here. I dug this out of my bag last night for when you asked me again how I can afford all this." She could see the moment her sister saw the numbers on her latest paycheck. When she finally looked up at her, Rogue took it from her and stuffed it back in her pocket. "That's for a single week, Lily. I told you, I make really good money because I'm very good at what I do. Then there are the other perks I get paid for as well. I want you to stop worrying about the money. Have a good time and buy the damned cheese."

Picking up the roll of cheese she'd been looking at, Lily put it in the cart. Then she turned to her. There were tears in her eyes, and if she started bawling again, they were all going to be bawling. It seemed that the little Fisher family was on the edge of it a great deal of late. Not that Rogue blamed them. There was shit enough for an army going on for them.

"I'm so proud of you, Rogue." She thanked her

sister. "I really am. You set out to do something, and you did it."

"I'd have not been able to do it if you'd not picked me up and shaken the shit out of me a few times back then. I would have been dead, literally, had you not gotten me cleaned up and off that shit when you did." Lily said she needed her. "Not nearly as much as I needed you then and now. You're all I have in the world with these kids. Let me have some fun with them before I have to go back out in the real world and take pictures of someone's idea of how they need to resolve something other than having a conversation."

"Is it bad for you sometimes?" Rogue only nodded. "They say you're the best. Even the FBI goes out of their way to make sure you have the best equipment. Of course, the article didn't say your name, but I knew who they were talking about. My little sister is a crime solver."

"Aunt Rogue?" Glad for the interruption, she looked at her new niece, Billy. The kid was beautiful. Extremely smart too, but painfully shy. She asked her what she needed. "I would like to ask you if I can get this. Now, don't tell me to just put it in the cart. I don't want to share it. I'd like to have it. After I read it, I'll share it, but I'd like to have it to read myself."

She took the book from her and looked at the cover. It was about husbandry, something she knew a little about but not enough to get her any kinds of points in joking about it. Rogue handed the book back to her.

"I would love to have you read this book. And you don't have to share if you really want to keep it. I don't see any of the others showing any kind of interest in that sort of thing, do you?" Billy blushed and shook her head. "I will tell you something. The family we're going to see, the Fosters? One of them, I don't remember his name right now, is a vet. A great one too, from what my friend says about him. While we're there, you can talk to him if you'd like. Quin. That's his name. Quin might even let you tag along with him on a few of his cases if you ask him nicely."

After hugging the book, Billy put it in the cart. Rogue had noticed that she was good at herding the kids around all the time, keeping them in line as well as helping out with the youngest, Sandy, when she got cranky or hungry. Rogue looked at her sister, asking her if she knew Billy had wanted that sort of book.

"I did. Before her father died, she'd been bringing home all sorts of animals. They followed her home, she'd tell us. But since then, I think because she knows there isn't the money for any extras, she's not been doing that." Rogue was going to see if she could hook Quin and her niece up as soon as she got there. "I'm going to have fun from now on. I might even buy myself something while we're here."

"Good." Her phone went off, and she looked at it. "Okay. Hold that thought. It's work. I have to take this. All right?"

"Yes."

She went outside to answer the call after handing her sister her credit card. The service was supposed to let the company know she could only take emergency calls while on vacation, so Rogue knew this had to be bad.

"I'm sorry, Agent Fisher, but there is a need for your services." She told the caller where she was. "That's another reason for this call. You're not too far from where we need you to be. The address is being sent to your phone, as well as all the information you're going to need to get there. Flight plans have been approved, and we'll need you to get to a place we're using to pick you up."

After getting the information, she told the caller — they didn't use names on that end — that she'd need to square away her family first. After being told she had about forty minutes, Rogue helped Lily and the kids load up the SUV they'd been using and talked to her sister.

"Everything you need to know to get to the Fosters is on the GPS. Just follow it, and it should take you about an hour to get there. I'll call Hi-Men when I get to the landing site." Lily asked her about that. "I'm going to be picked up in the parking lot right over there. The chopper will land long enough for me to get on it and out of here. You are going to be just fine driving to their home and making yourself helpful in what they're going to be doing for you. It will be just fine."

"I should wait for you." Rogue told her she didn't know how long she'd be. "Rogue, I don't know these people. I can't just barge in on them and expect them to be happy about it."

"They're thrilled, to be honest with you. Carmilla is Hi-Men's mother. She is excited to have kids around. Hop-Along is working on your case. I'm betting by the time I get back, they'll have you guys adopted, and you won't even need me around anymore." Lily told her that would never happen. "Thank you. I love you so much, Lily. Just go, have some fun, and let the kids have fun. You never know. You might just find someone to take them off your hands for a few hours so you can take a nap."

The helicopter landed just as she got to the sight. Hating to tell them bye, Rogue waved at them from the sky until the SUV was no more than a dot. Then she turned to her handler. Receiving a file from her, Rogue got into work mode. It was that or beg them to take her back to the site — she wanted her family back.

By the time she was in Columbus, Ohio, she had everything she needed to know in her head and on her computer. Her equipment had been put on-site for her to use, as well as two assistants she would need to help keep the notes she made. Things were progressing almost as soon as she was on site. However, as soon as she walked through the door of the abandoned house, she was ready to turn tail and run.

"It's bad." She nodded as she pulled on her coveralls. The man in charge, Agent Carlson, told her the things they knew so far. "Five dead. It was a bloodbath too. No one has been in the room except to check to see if there were any alive. We figured that out from the doorway but had to check. The officer who found them is outside. He's been sick since he got here."

"Did someone know to mark where they were touched?" He told her he had when he'd gone in, but the kid cop had puked in the corner. "Are you fucking kidding me? Not on the victims, did he? I will rub his face in his own guts if he did that."

"No, just in the corner. He seemed sort of afraid after he found out you were on your way. You scare the younger cops. Hell, you scare seasoned ones." She grinned at him. "You always think that is a good thing. It's not. Well, I guess it could be. He didn't lose his lunch on the body. Anyway, yes, they've been marked where we touched them. Since then, no one has entered."

She started away, then paused, looking at the

older man. "What is it you're not telling me? I haven't any idea why you'd think to save me from something, but tell me." He looked in the room, then back at her. "Tell me or not. I'm about to go in there, and you know how much— It's a baby, isn't it?"

"Yes."

She didn't want to go in there now. Knowing that she had to, she braced herself for whatever she would find when she got there.

"It's bad, I told you. Just do your thing, Agent Fisher, and we can all get the bastard or bastards that did this. All right. You can do this."

She rarely needed a pep talk when working— only when it was this bad. While she had done crime scenes before involving children, it was infants that really got to her. Badly. Taking a deep breath of clean air, she turned on her purifier and went into the room.

~*~

Pulling into the driveway, Lily sat there and looked at the house. None of the kids hopped out as she thought they might have. They could only stare at the "house" they'd been led to with the GPS directions in the car.

"Do you suppose it's an apartment building?" Lily told Gabe she didn't think it was. "Me either. It sure is a big one, don't you think? I mean, the garage is even bigger than the house Aunt Rogue was letting us use."

A man came out on the large wraparound porch and waited. Lily opening the car door seemed to be his que to come to them. As soon as she was out, not only did he shake her hand, but he picked her up in a large hug that had her slightly dizzy when he put her back on the ground.

"You've no idea how happy I am to finally meet you. I'm Loman Foster. My family is inside about to bust to come out and see you. Can they?" She told him sure, even as the front door opened and people poured out. She had a thought of one of those clown cars in the circus — there were so many of them. Sandy hid behind her. Donna, of course, stood in front of her and her sister.

"Donna, it'll be all right. These are Aunt Rogue's friends." She didn't move. "Donna, just be nice. They're not going to harm any of us. You heard what your aunt told you. They're big men, but not mean."

"It's all right." A man, as large as the car they were driving, got down on his knees in front of her daughter. "My name is Ronan. I'm Loman's brother. The other men here, for the most part, are our other brothers. You must be Donna."

"Aunt Rogue, she says I'm like her. Even though we're not blood-related." Ronan glanced at her, then back at her daughter. "You're a lion. She said we had better know that, but if we told anyone, she'd beat us with a wet willow stick until we were nothing but strips of meat. She's very descriptive about things."

"I guess she is." Ronan reached up and was handed a small bundle. Opening up the blanket the baby was wrapped in was all that was needed to get all the kids to his side. "This is my nephew. His name is Pete. We thought if you guys could see we don't hurt babies, you'd allow us to be your friends too."

"That's a really stupid reason to bring a baby to us, don't you think?" Lily was mortified, but everyone laughed. "Mom, you have to agree. I mean, what would you have done if I showed you a baby and told you I wanted you to like me? You would have…well, you would have taken it in too, even though we don't have two pennies to rub together. But sheesh, I don't think this was well thought out. Do you?"

"I don't know. Donna, I swear, you're more like your aunt daily." She put out her hand to shake Ronan's. "I'm Lily Fisher. This is my family. I guess you heard from Rogue? She sent us on so we'd not have to wait in the hotel forever for her to get finished."

Her car was unpacked, and their things were taken into the house even as she was gathering the kids up. Not only did they help her with the things they'd packed for this trip, but the men also took Rogue's car to the garage and put it away for her. She'd purchased the car on the road because it was insane to keep renting one. She liked this one better, and when she was working, Rogue was going to leave it for Lily to use. Lily was shown into one of the most beautiful bedrooms she'd ever been in and told she'd be there until they could figure out what to do when her sister returned.

Exhaustion had never been far away from Lily. She and it had been old friends since the day she'd been informed that her husband-to-be had been killed. Mark had been set to marry her, and she was going to adopt his children. He'd even gone so far as to put her on all his insurance policies as beneficiary, to receive the house as well as anything else he'd owned. Then Missy Tyler had stepped in and made their lives, all of them, a complete nightmare.

At the knock at the door, she wiped at the useless tears and asked the person on the other side to come in.

"I'm sorry, honey. Would you like me to come back?" She told the older woman she was all right. "I bet you have been holding on for some time now. Just let it out, and we'll hold you up. I'm here to tell you the children have been given swimsuits and are now out in the large pool. This house belongs to my son and his wife, Don and Brook. They're the ones that have the baby. Also, we heard from your sister earlier, and she said she'd call you later with some information. My goodness, you certainly have a wonderful family."

"I think so as well. Rogue, she's been taking care that they have a good time. I don't know what I'd have done without her." The woman reminded her that she was Loman's mother. "Yes, Mrs. Foster. I wanted to thank everyone for making us welcome here. It's been such a bad year or so for us. I hope your other son can help us."

"He will. And please, call me Carmilla. I know that you're not as trusting as we are, but if you'd like to take a lie down for a little while, we'll keep the kids entertained. I know how stressful it is to drive. I don't do it much anymore, but it can be nerve-wracking." Lily looked longingly at the bed. "Go ahead, dear. I'll make sure you're called in plenty enough time for dinner. We'll be cooking out, so that won't take a moment to finish. Go on, have a nice rest."

She did lie down, but she wasn't going to go to sleep. Lily promised herself she was only going to be there for twenty minutes or so, then she'd get up and see to her children. It was really nice of them to take care of them, but she wasn't going to take advantage of anyone. Not ever, if she could help it.

Just as she was getting up to see if she could find herself a book to read, her cell phone went off. Not recognizing the number, she didn't answer it. Bill collectors would either leave a message or not. She no longer cared about them hounding her.

The book she pulled off the shelf was a new

science fiction she hadn't read yet. Putting her feet up on the chair, Lily sat there admiring the room when her phone went off a second time. She'd been notified that whoever had called left a message, but she was enjoying herself too much to see what they had to say. She knew what she was behind on. Lily didn't need someone to remind her of it.

She was well into the third chapter of the book when someone knocked at the door. Lily jumped up, thinking that one of the kids might need her when she heard laughter from the doorway. It was Loman.

"I forgot." He leaned against the door and asked her if she had enjoyed herself. "I did, actually. I can't remember the last time I read even a want ad in the paper without anyone coming to get me. It was wonderful. But out of line. You must think I'm a terrible mother."

"What I think of you is that you're an amazing woman, and exactly like Rogue described you to be—a good person and a great mom. You have done an amazing job making things work out when you didn't have two pennies to rub together." Loman laughed. "Donna is the spitting image of Rogue. I don't know how that happened, but I love it. She's going to be a heartbreaker one of these days."

"Billy too. Oh, she wanted to talk to your brother. The one that is a vet. Rogue said she'd fix it for her. I didn't know she had thoughts of working in husbandry until this trip." Loman told her that Quin was out right now and would return in the morning. "I wouldn't have thought his sort of job would take all day. But then I've never had a pet in my life, so I haven't any idea how they work."

"Rogue told you we were lions, correct?" She nodded. "Good. I'm telling you that because there are currently six kittens in the barn that have been adopted by your kids. You can leave them here if you'd rather not take them with you."

"I don't even know where we're going." He said they had a home for them to use. "All this. I just don't understand any of it."

"What do you mean?" She told him. "We're being nice to you because you're a friend of my family. Not only that, but you're a nice person as well. Even if I didn't know your sister, I'd still think you're a wonderful human being. Just being around you makes me—"

He stiffened, and she knew one of her kids had been hurt. When she started around him, he stopped her with his hand. Loman told her that her kids were fine. It was Rogue.

"Is she hurt? Does she need me to come for her?" He said she was venting. "Oh. She does that very well too. I hope you don't get offended easily."

Loman shook his head while he still looked concerned. She followed him down the stairs, and when he pointed to the back doors, she headed that way so he could deal with Rogue. At the last minute, she ran back up the stairs to get her phone. Sending her sister pictures might cheer her up, she thought.

The kids were having a wonderful time. They had on swimsuits she'd never seen before but didn't mind. Once her sister returned, she'd ask for a loan and pay these kind people back. Her phone was ringing again just as she was getting the kids lined up in one shot. It was the same number. She also had four messages from it.

"Hello." She looked up at Cass when he sat down next to her on the decking around the pool. "I've been working on your case. I hope you don't mind me telling you, but you were royally screwed on it. I'm going to get back your home, money, and anything else I can take from that—" He looked around before he whispered "bitch" to her.

"Your mom is close—is that the reason for the whisper?" He nodded at her and grinned. "All you Foster men, you're very charming, aren't you? Rogue told me that you and Loman used to have so much fun when you were in college. Also, that women were always falling all over you. I can see why now."

An elderly woman in the ugliest bathing suit came and sat with her too. "My goodness, it does a person a good turn when there are children around, don't you think? I'm Jane Foster, this one's grandma. I was talking to him about your case earlier. My goodness, that woman needs to have her tits pulled up over her head." Lily couldn't help it, she burst out laughing. "I've been hanging around my granddaughters-in-law. Not too much, mind you, but it certainly has been fun learning new ways to insult someone. Those are the most well behaved children I've ever had the pleasure of meeting. You've done a good job with them."

"Thank you. They've made it very easy for me." She watched them playing while her phone rang again. "Someone is really wanting to talk to me. I've only just decided I'm not in the mood to be told how much I owe someone. I know I'm behind. It's why I've been working so hard." She looked at the two people at her little table. "I'm sorry. I don't know why I said that to you."

"You trust us. That's a good thing." Jane looked at the kids before getting up and going to the water again. "One thing you're going to find out soon enough is that we protect those we love. And I'm quickly falling in love with your little family here. You let Cass there see what the person wants, and he'll take care of them for you. Not a better attorney around, if you need one. Like I said, you can trust us for anything and everything, my dear."

The cannonball she did into the water made the kids laugh. She did too. Cass asked her if he could take care of her messages, and she nodded to him. Before he picked up the phone, however, she put her hand over his.

"We're not kidding about not having two pennies to rub together, Cass. I've been broke for so long I don't have any idea what I'll do if I ever get fixed again. The kids, they're all I focus on right now. They've gone without more than any child has. This money, it's not going to be to give us a better home, a nice car, or even a trip or vacation. It's going to put food on the table. Coats on them when it's cold. Shoes that I don't have to pick up at the secondhand store. We need this more than just for the money, but for us to feel like we're human again." He kissed her cheek as he picked up her phone. "What was that for?"

"You couldn't have said anything better to make me want to fight for you as hard as I can. Thank you." He walked away, putting in the code for the messages. However, he was only a few feet away when he returned. "This isn't from a bill collector, Lily. At least the first one isn't. It's from Missy Tyler. Do I have your permission to record these?"

"Yes. Do I want to know what she is saying?" He shook his head and told her not today. "Yes, at least not today anyway. Thank you for that. I didn't even know she had my number. Is it bad?"

"No. Don't think of it as bad. Just think of it as more information we can use in court. She was notified that we're taking her back to court. She's what you might call venting." She told him there was a lot of that going around today. "I heard. Rogue will be here sometime tomorrow. Loman is talking to her now."

Lily wanted to talk to her sister too. To tell her that things were moving along. But she also knew Rogue couldn't talk to her about her job, more than likely what she was venting about. The one and only time her sister had vented to her was bad enough. She didn't have any idea how Rogue was able to be as carefree as she seemed all the time and have to deal with the job she did.

When dinner was called, her kids got right out of the pool without complaint. She wanted to tell them they were great for not doing that when Billy sat beside her. Smiling big, she told her that since there was a pool here they could use all the time, they didn't have to hate getting out of it.

"I love you, Mom." Lily told her she loved her as well. "I know you do. I feel it in everything you do. The way you keep things from us when you're upset. But I wanted to tell you I don't just think of you as my stepmother. I don't know that I ever did after Dad introduced us to you. But you're my mother in all ways. Missy, what I plan on calling her from now on, was never there for me. Never came to my room at night and kissed me on the forehead like you do. She never worried over a temperature I had. Not one time did she ever go to something I was doing in school. You've been there for all of us when you really didn't have to be."

"Yes, I did." Billy shook her head. "Then you have to tell me why you don't think I need to be with you as much as I do."

"The moment my dad was killed, you could have walked away. You could have said, 'This is too much for a single person to take care of.' But you didn't. And when Missy took everything away from us, you—you didn't say it was too hard. That you had a son of your own that you needed to care for. That's another thing. You never treated us any different than you did Gabe, even though he's your biological son. I love you for that and so many other things I cannot even list. There are so many. You have given us more in the last few years than our biological mother gave us in all our lives. I love you for that and will forever. Mom. The word means so much more to me than it ever did since you've come into our lives."

When she walked away, Jane sat back down. She was crying, her beautiful cheeks red from them. When Jane blew her nose, she told Lily how much she had loved that. How, no matter what happened from now on, Billy and her other children had a place in her heart just as much as her other great-grandchildren. Then she left her there.

Lily was so touched that she had herself a good cry as well. They loved her. Not because they needed to, but because they wanted to. She wanted to hug them all up and hold them right then. But she knew it would embarrass them. Instead, she girded up her loins, as Rogue was so fond of telling her to do, and went into the house. Things were better. Not in any monetary way, but they were better for her all the same.

Chapter 2

Quin was never so glad to see his bed than he was tonight. It had been a long day and an even longer night with the animals he'd had to take care of at the Windle farm. It hadn't taken him long to discover that the animals, all of them, had to be put down. It was dealing with the children, who loved the animals, that had taken the most out of him. He had asked the mister why he'd waited so long to call him.

"Got no money, Doc Quin. That's the sad truth of it. Got us some insurance for the kids and all, but nothing out there for the cows and chickens. I surely do hate that you have to put them down, but there wasn't any way I was going to be able to afford to pay for meds for them when I got me five kids that need it more." He told him he still should have called him. "My missus, she told me I should have before it got so bad. But I knew you'd have to put them all down.

I knew in my bones that it would hurt the kids more than if I were to keel over and die myself."

The man had been heartbroken for his children. The cows, ten of them, had been too old to milk for some time, but the kids, he'd seen, had loved them too much to let them go to the butcher. Now there was nothing to do but burn the bodies and hope they'd find some other animal to love.

There had been seventeen chickens, ten cows, two horses, as well as a plethora of other farm animals, including a goat and a small lizard. The goat and the lizard had been saved, but nothing else. The infection had spread from animal to animal in less time than it would have taken for him to come out and get them vaccinated.

Before he left, he handed Mr. Windle all the cash he had on him.

"I can't take that from you. You done already came out here and did this for us, and I got no way of paying you." He told him it was for the children. To take them out for a pizza or something. "That would be fine. Right fine, I think." The man wiped at his tears with his handkerchief. "I'm a good man, Doc. I didn't mean for this to happen. But it just got away from me."

"I can see that, Mr. Windle. I've already made a couple of calls to Mr. Luma and Mr. Sheppard. They're going to cut out a couple of their cows for you to use as milkers. I've already been there to give them their vaccines. You make sure you call me for anything you might see. I'm not doing this as charity, I promise you. But I might need you some time to do something small for me, and I want to be able to depend on you. All right?" Windle nodded, looking at his kids. They were well mannered, polite, and cleaned up. They were also well-fed and good kids. It was one of the reasons he was helping him. "You come by the house sometime too. I know my momma would love to see you and your family. You know how she loves kids."

"She does. She did a good job raising you boys too, if you don't mind me saying, despite you having a bastard as a daddy." He told him he didn't mind. "Thank you, Doc. I surely do thank you from the bottom of my heart for this. You just call me. I'll help you in any way I can."

Now here he was, trying to make his body relax enough where he could at least get a couple of hours' sleep before he had to go and see his family. Not that it was a hardship to see them, but he knew there were some guests in town, and he didn't want to be in a bad mood because of his job. Beast, his cat, jumped up on the bed with him and got on his back. That, he thought, was what he needed, and he let sleep take him under.

When he woke, it was bright in his room. Thinking he might well have overslept and trying to work up the idea that he should be upset, he got up to take another shower. As he was letting the water just run over him, Loman spoke to him.

Are you all right? I heard what happened out at the Windle farm. That's not easy, I'm betting. He told him what he'd found when he got there. *I heard about it from his wife when she was here. I'm at your house, in the kitchen. You've got a cook now. I don't know which one of the sisters did it, but you do. Mrs. Windle sent you over six apple pies for your help. I'm being the best brother I can be and having a few slices of one of them for you. Throwing myself on that bomb, so to speak.*

Thank you ever so much. He laughed. Washing up, he stretched as he worked the shampoo out of his hair. *Have your friends shown up yet? I'm sorry I wasn't here to greet them. But duty called.*

Rogue's sister and her kids are here. Rogue, like you, was called away with work. She's going to be here sometime this afternoon. The FBI is bringing her straight here in one of their choppers. He asked what she did for them. *She photographs crime scenes. While that sounds like no biggie, she's really good at it. So good that when she asked them for a specialized camera to work with, they got it for her immediately. They use her photos in court, and no one disputes her findings.*

She sounds a good deal like you when it comes to taking pictures. Loman told him she was intense. *And you're not? I've seen you taking pictures of crap, Loman, and you're stiff as a board. I have no idea how when you take a picture, you can make it look so beautiful. You're very talented too.*

Thanks.

Quin turned off the water and grabbed a towel.

Sorry bro, but I'm going to take all the pies home with me. These are wonderful. I wonder if she's using Mom's recipe. I think I'm going to go and find someone selling blackberries, now that I think on it. I'd love a cobbler with some homemade ice cream. How about you?

Quin's belly rumbled, and he wanted one right now, with a huge scoop of homemade vanilla, his ice cream of choice. Getting dressed in a pair of shorts that were almost ready for the rag pile and a T-shirt from college, he made his way barefooted to the kitchen. True to his word, his brother was eating one of the pies.

"You're a pig." He didn't even bother denying it but nodded at him. Then he introduced him to his new cook. "Good to meet you, Mrs. Barclay. Do you know which person sent you to my home?"

"Brook Foster. She told me that any man worth his salt can cook, but there isn't any reason for it if he hires someone to wipe his butt too. She's a very vocal person, I think." They both laughed. "I'm glad to be here. All you men—she got cooks for the rest of you single brothers. Told me to tell you that so you could let your brothers know. I like it here. If I make you a list of stuff I'll need, how do I get it to you? Oh, my husband is going to do the butlering things for you. He likes being able to dress up, so you know."

They made arrangements for her to be able to order for his house. Quin didn't know how much to have her order, but he figured if she knew Brook, she had told her how. He was having his second slice of pie with whipped cream, the real stuff when he heard a helicopter go overhead.

If he'd not seen his brother when he heard it, too, he wouldn't have believed how his entire body had changed in that second. Excitement like he'd never seen before not only had Loman smiling, but he was nearly giddy with it. Standing up, he did a dance around the room and even danced with Mrs. Barclay. Loman asked him if he'd go with him to pick her up, and Quin not only said he would but nearly didn't change into something more presentable. Quin was putting on his shoes as he got in the car.

"Why are you in such a hurry? She's going to be here for a while, I guess." Loman told him how long it had been since he'd seen her. "I guess I can understand your excitement then. Seven years is a long time. But that means it's a solid relationship if you can get this excited about seeing someone after this long."

"Damn it." Quin asked him what was wrong now. "Ronan picked her up before I could. Now I have to share her with everyone else when I see her. He was taking the kids out for ice cream and heard her coming in. I'm to go to Don's house where her sister is."

Turning around, they headed back to town. It wasn't that far, but it was a good distance if you had to walk. Quin asked his brother if he thought Cass was going to win the suit for Rogen's sister.

"Yes. I do. He took a few phone messages for Lily earlier. Missy, that's the ex-wife's name, had called Lily. I went out and got her another phone, so she'd not have to hear what that woman is spewing at her. I guess she's really pissed off that Lily is going to try and get her things back. She threatened her to the point where she and the kids are going to hang out with one of us when they go into town now." He also told him about Billy, the oldest daughter. "It might just be a passing phase for her. I don't know a great deal about fifteen-year-old girls, but if you could take her with you or even to your office, it would be a great favor to me."

"Sure. I'd love to." He thought about having a girl at his office. While he didn't care one way or the other if someone wanted to tag along with him, he didn't want to have to put up with some girly girl in his office. He might even think of ways to let her see the dirtier side of veterinary care. "Have you thought of what will happen if this woman—either of them, I guess — turns out to be a mate for any of us?"

"I have given that a great deal of thought, as a matter of fact. I would be thrilled to no end to have one of you married to my best friend." Quin laughed until he realized Loman was serious. "What? You don't think you would like a woman who is a combination of Brook and Parker? Scary thought, I know, but you couldn't do any better than Rogue. She's about the most loyal and best friend I've ever had in all my life. And she saved my life."

"When?" He just shook his head. "You're going to have to tell me after saying that, Loman. I mean, was it a figurative saving or literal?"

"Literal. She saved my life, and I'll never be able to pay her back. She also got me on the right path to working in college. If not for her, I would have dropped out. That would have been a bad decision on my part. I have a lot to be thankful for about her. So does Cass."

Quin thought about that all the way to his brother's home. Whatever was going on with this woman, if she saved his family, he couldn't help but like her.

As soon as they pulled into the drive, Ronan was right behind him. The kids went to Rogue like they'd not seen her in years instead of only a few days. He got a kick out of the way she interacted with them too. She was no holds barred with them, telling them all she was back from the worst crime scene she'd been to in a long while. It took her hugging them and being dragged to the front of the house before he was able to follow. Christ, she was beautiful.

About halfway to the house, his cat felt trouble. Moving closer, looking around, it wasn't until Parker spoke that he understood the trouble was right in front of him rather than out in the open like he'd thought.

"Hello, Rogue. It's been a very long time." Rogue didn't move. Didn't speak either as she looked at Parker. "I've been trying to reach you. I wanted —"

"This is Parker? The one you were telling me about?" Rogue only nodded at her sister. "Rogue, I had no idea. I never knew what her last name was. She never mentioned it to me either."

"Why were you trying to reach me, Parker? Did you have more things you wanted to get out of me to tell the press? Or were you going for blood this time?" Parker told her she wanted to tell her she was sorry. "Too little too late, I'm afraid."

When Rogue turned to leave — that was all he could think she was doing — she knocked them both to the ground. When she landed on top of him, Quin knew his brother was going to be happy. Rogue was his mate. And she was spitting mad.

~*~

Pacing because she had no other outlet for her anger, Rogue kept staring at the man who was sitting in front of her. He was there to put some stitches in her leg that had opened up when she'd fallen on him. She wasn't sure how she felt about a vet putting stitches in her, but right now, she wanted to get out of there.

"You said you have a house." He told her he did. "And this house, does it have a back yard? One where no one will hear me if I were to scream and curse for about three days?"

"No one will hear you, no. Is this about Parker?" She growled at him, which usually worked with other people she was pissed off at. "I'm not sure if you're doing this because you're angry with me, but I didn't do anything wrong in this. I was just standing — "

"Parker hurt me. Not just mentally, though that was bad enough, but she went to the newspapers and told them I was a flake. Not that wording, but I nearly lost my job and all I'd been working for until then. She nearly ruined me." Quin told her Parker never went to the papers. "And how the hell would you know this? You weren't around when this happened. Or are you talking to her?"

"Yes, I'm talking with her and her husband. Apparently, Parker is crying, and it's bothering Don. Like it's bothering me that you're bleeding. If you'd allow me to either heal you or stitch you up, I'd feel so much better, as would my cat." She sat down on the couch and stood up again. "I'm not sure you're aware of this or not, but that wasn't nearly enough time to get you sewn up."

"I'm well aware of it. Let's go to your house." He stood up to follow her, and she was surprised when he said they could walk to it. "I thought you said no one would hear me if I were to scream and rant."

"They won't. I have a couple of deep caves I thought you might want to use. That way, I can hit you over the head with one of the stones so I can fix you up." She stopped and stared at him. Asking him if he'd just made a joke, he looked like he was thinking on it. "I guess I was. I don't usually go for jokes when I'm upset. And I am. So is my cat. So, shall we get going?"

"I should talk to Parker. Your family, they're being really good to me and my family, and I need to tell her off. I won't, just so you know, because I'm not stupid, but I should." Quin didn't move toward her or even order her to do what she had said. "You're weird. I know I might have said that to you earlier, but you are weird. Not like Hi-Man weird. Because he is too, but just strange."

"Hi-Man?" He laughed. "I didn't know you called him that. You know Cass too, I'm to understand. What do you call him?"

She told him. "He was so uptight in college. I thought joking around with him would get the rod out of his fucking ass. I don't like this one bit, so you know. Just because I'm willing to go to your house, it doesn't mean that I'm going to lay down and spread out for you. Get it?" He laughed, and she didn't know if she wanted to punch him in the balls or laugh with him. "I've had a really terrible few days. I can't tell you about it—it's my job, you see."

"I will never tell anyone, not living or dead, what you share with me. On my honor as a brother to the king of lions." She was impressed that he didn't hesitate in telling her that. And for whatever reason, she believed him. "You tell me about your day, and then I'll tell you how I had to go to a farm to kill all their animals because they were too fucking poor to come to see me before it was much too late to save them."

"I'm sorry." He nodded and then sat down on the ground. She joined him, but not close enough that he could touch her. Rogue didn't know what she'd do if he were to show her some kind of emotion along with hers. "They were, for all outward appearances, a normal family. They had two lovely children and an infant. She was only three days old. I wonder what sort of sins—because what else could it have been about an infant?—would cause them to murder her like they did."

"People—humans, for the most part—don't have a lot of logic most of the time. Shifters either, but most of the ones I know usually have other means of taking care of their bad days. I run. Far and fast." He picked up a stone and bounced it on his hand, front then back. Front then back. "My father was one of the first group. He was a son of a bitch right up until the day he was killed. Tell me the rest, Rogue. I want to help you."

She could see the crime scene now. Every time she closed her eyes, it was there. It was why she came home today instead of tomorrow, as the police and Feds wanted her to. She needed her nieces and nephews. Needed her sister to hold her and tell her it was going to be all right. But she'd met Quin and Parker instead.

"The little boy was at the bottom of the bed when he was murdered. The father killed him. Took a chainsaw and ran it from the top of his small head to his groin, splitting him in half. He was still lying there when I arrived, like some morbid art project that was still wet. The little girl must have run because one of the parents hit her at the doorway to the closet. She was killed before she was split open the same way." She thought about what she was going to tell him next. About finding the baby like she had. "The people I work with, they know I don't do well when there is a child involved. I do the work anyway because I'm good at what I do, but they couldn't have prepared me for this. No one, not even after being told, would have been ready to see that the baby had been cut into four pieces. Her small body, barely formed, was strewn around the bedroom like they swung her from the fan above."

She started crying then, hard sobs she'd been holding inside since she'd found the room. Her body ached with the need for justice. Her heart hurt so badly Rogue was sure it would never mend.

Quin picked her up then. Held her in his arms as he moved them across the yard. He never once told her to stop crying. He didn't make fun of her either, as she had expected. All he did was hold her tightly to his chest and in his arms as he moved them to a place where he could sit down. There, once she was tightly consumed by his compassion, Rogue let go of all the fears, the pain, all of her sickness of the human way of dealing, and cried loud, long and painfully.

At some point, she must have fallen asleep. Waking but not moving, she watched as Quin spoke to someone she couldn't see. It occurred to her that she was listening in on his conversation when he looked down at her with a grin.

"It's all right, Mrs. Barclay. She's awake now. Go ahead and make us some dinner if you don't mind." The lady laughed and said she'd do that, and Rogue heard a door behind her slide shut. "How do you feel? I have this terrible crick in my arm, so don't move. If you do, I'm going to whimper like a kid, and then how will I be able to be all macho and manly with you?"

"Tell me where it hurts, and I can try and ease off it." He pointed to his shoulder, and she moved her head just enough to see him wince. "I'm sorry. You must think I'm some sort of fruit cake for sobbing like this, then putting you in pain when I just fall asleep like I don't have a care in the world."

"I didn't think that at all. I would say—though I don't know you well enough just yet to be sure—that you've been holding that in for some time." She nodded and inched her way off his arm more. "I'm not going to ask you why you do it. I completely understand loving a job that makes you ill one moment then will take you to the halls of hell the next. You told me you were good at it. I think you're better than good at it. You're the best there is."

"I don't know that I'm the best, but I do help close a lot of cases." She moved off his arm and to the floor of the deck. When he stretched his arm over his head, she heard it pop twice before he smiled at her again. "Your family must think I'm the worst kind of person."

"No. But I have been talking to Parker. She wants you to talk to her. Parker doesn't understand what you meant when you said she would go to the press again. I'm not taking sides, mind you, but she is genuinely confused at that." She told him what had happened. "I don't think it was her."

"So much for not taking sides." He pulled her back to him when she started to rise. "She did it. That's what I was told at the newspaper. Parker told them I was a flake. That I took other people's ideas and claimed them as my own. She nearly ruined me when she did that. It took me a long time to even want to face people again. Parker—"

"Was in prison for the last eight years." Rogue asked him what he'd said. "She had been falsely accused of killing her father and was in prison for the last eight years. She only just got out right before meeting my brother. She's looking into it now to see who would have pitted the two of you against each other. Did you know her before all that happened?"

"No. I mean, I'd heard of her. Who wouldn't have heard of a witch? I have to admit, I never believed it. Is she? A witch, I mean?" He said she was the strongest witch there ever was. "Figures. She'd be the one that would be able to turn me into a frog. Will she?"

"No, not now that you're a part of my family." They both turned when Parker spoke behind them. "I'd like us to start again, you and I. To be honest with you, Rogue, I didn't know anything about you and your secondary job until I started looking into what you said to me. Hell, I didn't know you at all before that until I heard you were coming here. Imagine my surprise when I saw that not only were you a famous artist, but you worked for the Feds as well. Then I found the articles about how I had told a tabloid about your stealing work and forging your name on it. Why didn't you tell them you only signed your first name, and there wasn't any way that you did the art they were talking about?"

"I didn't want to put it out there that someone hurt me." Parker said she was stupid for that. "Thanks. You the welcoming committee here, or do they have more people that can insult and knock me around?"

"Just me for now." Parker laughed when she smiled at her. "I am sorry, Rogue. I had no idea that someone did this to you. It didn't hurt me one way or the other, as I was already in prison, but I promise you that I'm looking into it right now. I'm also helping Cass with your sister's money. That was terrible what they did to her."

"Missy Tyler." Parker asked her what her maiden name was. "Let me think. I don't know for sure, but I think it was Storm. Or Stormy. Lily would know. Why do you ask?"

"It helps. All the little bits and pieces I can weave together help me take a clearer picture of the person I'm trying to figure out. Like, is she Missy or Melissa? How does she spell it? It's not a precise thing, digging into her past, but it helps me focus on her when I have everything in a neat row." Parker and the rest of them went into the house when they were called to dinner.

"I'm a witch, you've heard that. What you might not know is that I can find and work with people that I don't have to touch or meet. But it doesn't do me much good to find them if it's the wrong person. Or if I don't have the kind of information that helps me look for what I'm searching for."

"I have her address." Parker laughed and said that would certainly narrow it down. "Yeah. My sister and Mark Tyler lived there with their kids up until his death. I liked him. He was ambitious, friendly, and he treated his kids with respect but with a firm hand. Much like Lily did with Gabe."

"Where is Gabe's father? Is he in the picture?" Rogue told her that Lily and Ben were just kids when she found out she was going to have his baby, and they separated as friends. Then he got married himself. "So he's not wanting to take Gabe."

"No. Don't jump to conclusions that make people look bad. That's my job. Ben takes him once a year for the summer. Not this year, however. Not because he didn't want to, but he couldn't. His mother got very ill and had to move in with them, which I guess is just as well. I don't think Lily would have been able to afford to send him anyway. It was her turn to buy the tickets." Rogue thought about it. "I'm not sure how well she might be getting along in this without the kids. Having them all around her is what gives her the strength she needs to get going every day."

They enjoyed a nice dinner. There were thick steaks to eat, something she didn't indulge in too often, and a wonderfully tossed salad. Rogue loved salad and would eat it exclusively if she was given the chance. But she also knew she needed the protein and mixed meat with her salad intake when she could.

Rogue realized that no one brought up anything heavy at dinner. There was no talk of jobs, money, or the impending things coming up with Lily and her family. As soon as they were seated in the living room, however, they spoke of everything. Not just the good, but the bad things as well.

It occurred to her that this was their way of letting off steam. While she held Pete, the cutest little guy she'd seen in a while, she thought of the things that had happened today. And suddenly, it didn't seem so bad. It was, she thought, but it wasn't weighing on her as it usually would.

Looking over at Parker, she saw the other woman wink at her. She wondered if Parker had anything to do with the stress being easier to handle. Whatever it was, her or the family around them, she was going to take it. It was the first time in a very long time she felt like a person and not consumed by a lot of things she really had no control over.

Of course, she still had to deal with Quin and what he might want from her. But she had a feeling he wasn't like most males she knew. Not all men, but even humans wanted more than just wives—they wanted someone to do things for them. But neither Quin nor his brothers seemed the demanding type. Rogue supposed that time would tell. She was looking forward to seeing what came from this deal as his mate.

Chapter 3

Missy wanted to find Lily and beat the ever-loving shit out of her. What did she think to gain by taking her back to court? Nothing, that was what she was going to get. Not one damned thing. It would take money to come after her, and she'd made sure the little twit didn't have any.

"Did you hear what I said to you?" She waved her hand at the butler that had been there since she and Mark had lived there. "All right then. Since I know you can't stand to have things repeated to you, you have a lovely day, missus."

When he stepped out of the room, she let out a huge sigh of relief. Missy didn't like dealing with people. Actually, she didn't care for anyone but herself, and sometimes she couldn't even stand herself. Getting up to pour herself a drink, the grandfather clock chimed. Smiling, she drank the drink down, considering it her breakfast.

The phone rang somewhere in the house. Why there was a house phone in this day and age was something she never understood. But when it went unanswered, she wondered at that. Then there was an insistent ringing at the front door. Again, it didn't get answered.

Vowing to go after the one that was supposed to do that for her, she opened the door and nearly fell off her heels when the door opened much easier than she thought it would. While she was trying to gather up her composure, the person on the other side of the door laughed. That was when Missy looked in her direction.

"Deliveries are to be made at the back door. Remember that the next time or I'll have your job." The woman said something, but Missy didn't understand her. Asking her to repeat herself got her more laughter.

"I said, you'd better be looking for some sort of job, so when you're kicked out of here and have to repay the money you took, you'll have something to fall back on. Are you Melissa Strum Tyler?" Nodding, she realized that this person knew her maiden name when even she barely remembered it. "Here you go. You've been served."

The packet—there was no other word for the thick envelope—hit her in the chest. The woman hadn't moved to give it to her that she'd seen. Not only that, but as soon as Missy looked up from the thing she'd been given, the woman was gone, like she'd never been there. Had it not been for the thing being in her hands, she might well have believed it was all a drunken aberration.

"Not that I'm drunk. It is only nine in the morning." She really didn't have any idea of the time. The stupid clock only chimed every fifteen minutes — for all she knew, it could have been nine in the evening. "Why does it get dark sometimes in the evening, and other times it doesn't? Stupid weatherman."

Taking the envelope to the living room, she laid it on the table with all the other mail she'd been getting from the mailbox the last few days. Her attorney had advised her to keep everything in one place, so she was. He'd also sent her a certified something or another, which she ignored as well. He more than likely was reminding her again to keep her shit together.

When she started to get hungry, she called out for Carl. Carl didn't like her. She didn't care for him either, but since he was being paid to wait on her, she tolerated him. Yelling again, hating that her voice sounded slurred, she finally went to where the staff hung out and entered the kitchen.

Missy didn't know what she had expected to find when she entered the only room in the house that she'd never made a habit of going into. But finding all the cabinet doors open, showing the empty cavernous shelves, she wondered if there was something she should be aware of. Was there a delivery of some kind coming in? But the cabinets were devoid of even the simplest of things. Not that she had a good idea of what she should have found in cabinets, but there should have been chips or something, she thought.

Looking around for something, an order that was coming or a note to tell her what was going on, she found an envelope with her name on it. Opening it up, she smiled when she saw that it was written out to Mrs. Tyler. Then she got to the body of the letter.

Mrs. Tyler. We have decided to take what you owe us in past wages from the household. There is no reason for you to call the police, as they were here when we took what we felt was owed to us. We did try, on several occasions, to talk to you about this, but you refused to listen.

She'd just see about that. Taking out her cell phone, she was dismayed to find that she had no service. Missy wasn't sure what was going on, but she was going to get to the bottom of it right now.

I'm to inform you that you should read the paperwork you received via courier yesterday. In it, you'll find the information you'll need about your banking, as well as any outstanding payments that haven't been paid. There was a happy face drawn there that she thought was highly inappropriate. *You have a good day, Mrs. Tyler.*

This couldn't be happening to a better person if you ask me.

"Well, that was nice." She laid the letter down just as the lights went off. Getting up to turn the switch back on, she clicked it several times before she concluded she'd blown a fuse. "Like I have any idea how to go about changing a fuse."

The rest of the house was just as dark. Going to the living room where all the paperwork she'd received over the last week was laying, she started sorting out things that were *personal* — it bothered her that there were so few of them — *past due* and *final notice*. Then she came to the thick thing she'd gotten just this morning.

Opening it up, she not only broke one of her nails, but she also got a papercut. The stupid thing was sealed up like it held national secrets, she thought. Once she was able to get a tissue on her bloodied finger and tape on her nail, she began reading what had been the cause of so many things she'd have to take care of today.

It read like instructions in putting something together. Not only that, but it was like it wasn't in a language she even understood. It was in English, but it read like — "A divorce paper."

Getting to a better place where she could spread things out, she put the paperwork on the dining room table. There it was, she saw — she was being sued. Not only that, but her bank accounts had been frozen, all her credit cards had been cut off, and even any kind of vehicle she might have driven was no longer there for her to use.

Missy needed to call her attorney. How she was going to manage that, she didn't have a clue. Going to the neighbors seemed her best bet, but in the time she had lived there with Mark and now, she didn't have any idea who they were. She hadn't wanted anything to do with them in all this time.

Getting dressed, she had to change her clothing three times before she felt like she could go out and face the neighbors. All the time she was working on making herself look presentable, she tried to come up with a good excuse as to why she needed to use their phone. The power was out sounded the best, but that would only work until the person could see that the rest of the neighbors had power and she was the only one without.

Then there was the added trouble that she didn't know any phone numbers. She'd gotten into her phone only to find out she didn't remember the attorney's name. After finding one number that had the distinguished title of being called "Fucker," she figured it was him. If it wasn't, she didn't know what she was going to do.

When she was finally ready to go, she noticed the woman from this morning was standing at the end of her driveway. Missy asked her if she had a phone she could borrow.

"I do not." She asked her if she had a phone. "Oh, I have a phone. But none that I care to let you borrow. Are you going somewhere, Melissa? Are you having issues you need help with?"

"What do you know about this?" The woman just smiled at her. "Listen. If you're not going to be helpful, then I'd like for you to leave me alone. I have better things to do today than to banter with someone who is getting too much pleasure out of my woes."

"Your 'woes,' as you called them, are about to get a great deal worse, I'm afraid. Well, not afraid, since I'm having way too much fun at your expense. But the neighbor, the one you think is going to lend you a phone, she's not home. I made sure of that for you." Missy asked her why she'd do that to her. "Why? Because I don't like you. Not one bit. Not to mention, you're not a nice person."

"Why would you say that? You have no idea who I am." The woman just smiled at her. "Whatever. Stay out of my way, or I'll mow you down like I do people that get into my way. Stupid people mostly."

Missy decided she'd walk into town. She had no reason to believe the woman standing in her drive, but for some reason, Missy had a feeling the people next door were indeed gone. Not that she had anything to do with it, but they wouldn't be home, and she had had enough of wasting her time today.

It wasn't such a bad walk. Missy enjoyed the fresh morning air as well as the smells that came from people mowing their lawns and such. Since she didn't know anyone that nodded or waved at her, she did the same back to them. It was something she knew about, having grown up in a small town before marrying Mark.

Mark had been her way out. Missy had liked him well enough. He was a nice man, handsome as well as ambitious. He had courted her, wooed her in a way that made her heart strings pull. But she'd known she would never love him. Missy didn't love anyone but herself.

She wasn't stupid either. Graduating at the top of her high school class, she'd also excelled in college. Missy was going to be able to hold a conversation with someone and not just nod and smile. That had been her mother. Mom had been a good wife to her father, but she was also incredibly naïve and dumb when it came to social gatherings. Missy was smart enough to watch the other women and learn from them.

Not that she hated her parents. She'd loved them very much—as much as she was capable of, anyway. Her dad had died when she was seventeen. Her mother had taken it badly and had to be put into a nursing home until she passed away when Missy had been married to Mark. Her parents went out of the world much the same way they'd lived it, without much of a fanfare nor any kind of sadness.

The police went by her on her way into the hardware store, the only place she saw that advertised that they had a public phone. Getting seated in the back of the building, she laughed at the way someone had attempted to decorate the little room. There were fresh flowers in a small vase, as well as several pads of paper and two pens for her to use. Pulling out the phone number, she began dialing it — it was a real rotary phone. Dialing the number, Missy hoped she not only had the right number but would be able to get someone to help her with the trouble she was having with Lily.

Telling the person who answered the phone what she needed, she was put on hold three times, repeating her story each time she was transferred to someone else. Missy knew better than to piss anyone off at an attorney's office. If they took exception with her, she might well end up with the worst partner or under-attorney they had. So she smiled and was polite each time she had to repeat the reason she was calling.

"Ms. Tyler, this is Wayne Donaldson." She didn't know him from anyone else she'd spoken to, so she asked if he could help her. "I was your attorney when you sued Ms. Fisher for your ex-husband's estate. After the verdict was read, my firm decided we could no longer be your attorneys. We also found out some things afterwards that were not on the up and up when we went to trial for you."

"I just need you to tell me what this new thing is saying to me. It's something about my accounts being sealed up." He said he knew about her being served, but he could no longer help her. "Not even to tell me what this says? I'm not stupid. I'll have you know. I just don't understand all these therefores and such."

"I'm sorry. This firm isn't going to be able to help you in any way." She started to hang up when something else occurred to her. Missy asked him if he was going to be in the courtroom on the day she was supposed to be there. "Ms. Tyler, we are no longer client and attorney. I cannot in any way answer your questions about anything to do with the upcoming court appearances you might have pending."

The line went dead. She didn't know for sure, but Missy thought this entire thing had to do with that stupid cow, Lily. There wasn't any other name for the woman but stupid cow, as she had let Missy not just take her home and money but saddle her with three kids that were no more hers than they were the attorney's.

She had to think about what to do now. Going to the bank was her first order of business. She knew her accounts had been frozen, but she did have money in her safety deposit box for emergencies like her hair needing done or a small trip.

Going there next, she was waiting to talk to the banker when the police walked in. They didn't speak to her, just hung around the front of the place like they were expecting someone like John Dillinger or Bonnie and Clyde to come rushing in. When her name was called, she moved into the office. The police followed her.

"Is there something going on that I need to know about, gentlemen? I'm only here to get into my safety deposit box. Is that a crime now?" Neither of them said a word. "The talkative types, are you? Well, I don't know what is going on, but I think you should be out solving real crimes, like why my power has been turned off, rather than harassing someone like me when I've done nothing wrong."

"We're here for two reasons, Ms. Tyler." The officer made her name sound like something he'd stepped in outside, and it was smelling up the room. "One, we're here to inform you that you're not going to be able to take anything out of the bank. That would include safety deposit boxes. The second thing is, your home has been ceased by the FBI, for a number of reasons, but one of them is bribing a judge."

Arguing with a cop was like arguing with a waitress. While the waitress would spit in her food, a cop would find every reason he could, mostly made up ones, to get her into a cell, a place she'd not be able to get anything done from. And Missy had plenty to get going on today.

"What am I supposed to do without any money or a place to live? Have you thought of that?" He said he was hoping she'd do something dumb and he'd have to arrest her. "I won't even dignify that with any kind of response. You'll be hearing from my lawyer. This is not the way to treat someone. I don't care for you going around telling people I've bribed a judge either. You'll be sitting in your own jail cell soon, young man."

As she left the bank, she thought about how much cash she had on her and realized it was as much as she'd gotten out of the bank today — zip. There were a few dollars in the house, nothing more than about fifty bucks. But she knew from her friends, once you were locked out of your house by the Feds, you were out no matter what.

She honestly thought about doing something dumb, just so she'd have a roof over her head and some food in her belly. But to admit to anything, including not knowing where her next meal was coming from, wasn't going to happen. Missy thought she was hiding it very well that she was upset. However, inside of her, she just needed one more thing to go wrong for a full-blown screaming fit to take place.

~*~

Quin didn't think he'd ever enjoyed himself as much as he was at the moment. Billy was having fun, but she was seriously working with him. Not only did she not mind getting dirty and covered in things best left on the ground, but she also seemed to do it all with a smile on her face.

"Okay, now, you have to be careful when you walk around a horse. Especially one that doesn't feel well. The best way to approach him is to make sure he knows you're around, and you don't mean to cause him any harm." She nodded and walked to the front of the horse. Quin watched her as she spoke softly to the horse and told him how sorry she was that he wasn't feeling well. "Good. Let him get a smell of you too. I know that sounds silly, but he'll be able to smell your fear or anger. Just let him see you're here just for him and that you want to help him."

"Good boy." She put her forehead on that of the horse. "Do you know Doc? Well, he's teaching me some things I'd like to know about when I get older, like helping animals like you. I know you hurt, big boy, but I promise you, if anyone can fix you up, it'll be Doc. All right? You just let us work on you, and you'll be running around in the grass in no time."

They talked, Billy, speaking to the horse, Shire and Shire making his noises at her. When Quin got to the sore spot on his leg, Shire huffed but didn't kick out like he had expected him to do. The entire time, Billy was telling him how good he was doing and that Doc was going to fix him.

"I see you got yourself an assistant there, Doc. She sure is a pretty little thing." Robin Quarter was the owner of the horse. It bothered Quin when Shire moved away from him like he was fearful of the human. "Me and Shire here, we got off on a bad place yesterday. He didn't want to listen, and I had to make him."

"You hit him? Is that why he has that sore place on his leg?" Quin started to tell Billy he had this when she went into full protective mode on him. "What is wrong with you? Hitting something that outweighs you and thinking he'd not get you in the end. He kicked you too, didn't he? Well, good for him. Holy mother of pearl, you don't anymore deserve an animal than that tree does. I have a good mind to tell someone on you. Beating a poor animal like you have. You're going to be lucky if we don't have to remove his leg the way you've treated him."

"You think that might happen, Doc?" Quin wisely said nothing as he worked on the laceration that went all the way to the bone. "Christ. I can't afford that. My daddy is going to have a fit as it is that I had to call you out here already."

"Perhaps you should have thought of that before you pulled a whip out and began beating him. Shire is a good horse, and you more than likely ruined his chances of a good life, you moron." Robin stepped towards Billy. Before Quin could move to save her,

Billy lifted her chin up and spoke in a soft yet scary voice. "Go ahead and hit me, you dumbass. If you do, not only will I own this horse, but I'll go straight to the press and tell them you beat your animals into submission."

"Robin, walk away from the young lady." Mr. Quarter came into the barn where they were. Not only did Robin not move, but he looked as if he might go ahead and hit Billy anyway. "You heard me, son. Get out of here now while you still can. Because I know for a fact you don't want to fuck around with this child any more than you do Doc here. Get going."

When Robin walked away, Mr. Quarter, Robby, asked about the horse. Quin told Billy to explain to him what had been going on. She not only told him his son was an abusive man but that he should be whipped with the same whip he used on the horse. Quin was laughing by the time Robby sat down across from the two of them as they worked.

"He gonna lose that leg, Quin?" He said if it was kept clean and no one stressed him out anymore, he'd be fine. "This isn't the first time you've been called out here for this sort of thing, is it? Don't give me that 'it's your job' thing either. I pulled up the file on your billing. You ain't been paid, have you?"

"No, sir. But I'm doing all right. And I knew if it came to it, I could go ahead and ask you for it. But I'm all right." Robby looked at Billy, who was now wrapping the wound on Shire's leg. "To answer your question, no, this isn't the first time I've been out here to stitch up one of his messes. Two weeks ago, not only did I put seventeen stitches in one of your ponies, but one of the hands needed several too. Robin is mean with that whip."

"You should have beat him more as a kid." Billy didn't look at either him or Robby when they turned to her. "I have an aunt that could teach him a few lessons about being nice to something that depends on you. For that matter, I have an entire family that will gladly take him to task if you want. You say the word, Mr. Quarter, and they'll be right on his butt."

Robby laughed. It sounded like he was caught off guard by it in much the same way Quin had been. Billy was just like Rogue, he was finding out—a spitfire, and not at all backward in saying what needed to be said. He'd have to tell her family she wasn't in any way backward or shy. She was right up in your face, ready to tell it like it was.

"This one of your new family, Quin?" He told him she was his mate's niece. "She's a keeper, I tell you. I wish I had five just like her." He looked at Billy, who was cleaning up the mess they'd made, as well as making sure all the blood and needles were cleaned or packed away. "I tell you what, young lady. I'd like to hire you to come out here a couple of days a week. I think you'd make a good foreman for my horses here.

I'd like to tell you I think you could take over now and not miss a beat, but I think you have to be a tad older for me to do that. But you come out here three days a week, and I'll personally teach you everything there is to know about horses and breeding."

"I'd have to ask my mom." Robby said that was a good girl. "Mr. Quarter, I'd have to be able to work here without your son hurting me or the horses. I'm enjoying this, working with Doc Quin, but it has always been a dream of mine to work with racers."

Quin hadn't known that, but he could see it. Also, the hope in her eyes and face told him that for her to turn down this opportunity would be like sticking him in a cell without sunlight or air. He promised her he'd bring her and pick her up — if her mom agreed.

Mr. Quarter showed her around the barn. The quarter horses were world-renowned for their speed and beauty. The man owned nearly seven thousand acres, all of it devoted to not just a place to house his prized animals but to keep them in shape, train them, and keep them healthy. Quin had been asked — no, begged — to be his full-time vet for years. This was the first time he could ever remember considering the position.

On the way back to the office, Billy didn't say much. She was a thinker, much like her mom. It surprised him every time he thought of her family that they weren't biological. The more he was around them all, the more he realized it was only blood that separated them. They loved as fully and as passionately as he did his family.

He was pulling into the office when she finally turned to him. "Are you upset with me?" He asked her why she thought that. "Because I got mouthy with Robin. I know his dad thought it was funny, but I think I embarrassed you."

"No, you didn't. I was very proud of you for standing up to him. But I do want to warn you not to do that when it's just the two of you. He's a mean man." She nodded and looked at his building. "Robby was serious about the job, Billy. And I'm seriously considering taking the one he offered me as well. Is that all right?"

"I would like to have someone there I can depend on. I believe Mr. Quarter will go out of his way to make sure I'm safe, but I know you will no matter what." He said he would. "I don't want to ask my mom. I mean, I want to, but I don't want her to turn me down. I think that with you working there with me, she might consider it more. But I hope that's not the reason you take the job."

"No, it's not. I've been losing money around town because no one needs a vet any more than they need to have their cars broken down. I'll still help out around the town. It would be my pleasure. And I did speak to Robby about that. He was fine with it." Billy nodded, still not looking at him. "Billy, what is it? What are you thinking about that has you so tensed up?"

He could tell that whatever was bothering her, she was struggling with it. Wanting her trust, he waited until she was ready. As far as he was concerned, Quin had nothing to do but help this child with whatever was bothering her.

"When I was a little girl before my dad died and while Missy was still at the house, a man came by with a horse he was selling. I have no idea why he stopped at our house to ask if we could buy it for a few dollars. Everyone in town knew Missy didn't like people. But he asked." Quin wondered what had made the impression on the child when she turned and looked at him. "I couldn't keep the horse. I knew better than to ask for him. But I borrowed money from my dad, and took my birthday money and gave it to the man. He cried so much that it hurt me too. My dad found out and said it was a good thing I'd done, and he didn't want me to pay him back. I knew, you see, that the man wasn't just hungry, but that he'd been feeding the horse and going hungry himself. That horse, the one he was selling? It spoke to me. I don't mean in words like I use, but in images."

He believed her. Quin wasn't sure why he did, but he thought it wasn't just horses she could speak to, but all animals. It would be her main reason for wanting to help him, he'd bet. Thinking about how to talk to her, he figured the straight-up approach would work better than anything with her.

"You can speak to them too?" She nodded slowly. "All right. So today, when you were helping me with Shire, he told you something. Do I need to know?"

"Yes. Robin stole him from another horse farm." There was more. Quin knew it but waited. "He killed the man that was in the barn with Shire, as well as three other horses. It's what made me so mad at Robin in the first place."

"The dead man. Do you know if he was found or not?" She shook her head. "I'm not going to like this, am I?"

"No. He fed him to the pigs. I know this because they told Shire, and he told me." Christ, he thought. This was by far more than he'd imagined when he asked her about this. It was good information, but now what did he do with it? "I've not told anyone but you, Uncle Quin. I was afraid they'd think I was lying."

"Not my family. Here is what we'll do. I'll talk to your aunt first, then my family. You need to tell your mom what you can do. All right? That way, we can work in the open with this information and not have to sneak around."

"I will." She hugged him, and he hugged her

tightly. "Thank you so much, Uncle Quin. I knew I could talk to you about stuff, but this is freaky, don't you think?"

"Honey, I'm brother-in-law to a witch. I can change into a lion, and my brother is the king of lions. Now you can talk to animals. Nothing about this is freaky so much as it's par for the course." She laughed, which was what he'd hoped for. "We'll take care of this, Billy. I swear to you. Even if I have to shift into my lion and kill him, we'll get through this."

He wasn't sure how, but he figured he'd go to the one person that would know how to handle this the best. Getting out of the car, he reached for his grandma. She'd either tell him to go kick some ass, or she'd help him. Either way, he'd welcome the help.

Chapter 4

Unsure of what to do with the information, Rogue stared at her glass of water. Jane had been with her when Quin had asked to speak to her, and she told him to come home and do it. That whatever he had to talk about, his mate needed to hear it as well.

"Well, what do you think we should do?" Quin wasn't being pushy like she might have been had she delivered the news to him, but she wasn't ready to give him what was racing around in her head just yet. He seemed to understand that and turned to his grandma. "You should have seen Billy standing up to Robin. She didn't hold back at all. Had I closed my eyes for a moment, I would have sworn it was you or Mom there. Or Rogue. She got right up in his face too. Then she told Robby he should have beaten Robin more as a kid."

"I wish I could have seen his face. I bet Robby

hasn't been spoken to like that since his missus passed on. Now there was a woman that could get up in a person's face. She'd not suffer fools well. Also, she would have beaten Robin more." He'd not known that Robin's mom had passed away in childbirth. "I'm glad he is giving that child an outlet for her gift. She does think of it as a gift, doesn't she?"

"We didn't talk about it much, other than her telling me she's had it since she was a child." Rogue asked him if she'd told him any other things about animals. "No. Just the horse named Shire. I do believe she can talk to more than just horses, but she was a little skittish, so I didn't press her on that. What do you think her mom will do?"

"She'll take it well. I don't know why, but I have a feeling Lily will have had some indication that Billy could do something special anyway. She's hinted about— So the horse was contacted by the pigs to let him know the man in the barn was dumped by Robin to be eaten so no one would find his body. Even out loud, that sounds like I'm off my rocker. I don't want you to think I don't believe her, but it is a far stretch from being a shifter to an animal whisperer." Quin nodded at her and told her she was doing well. "Thanks. But you're not going to get any brownie points with this. This is big news, and someone is going to have to go to Mr. Quarter and let him know that some pigs told his horse, who told my niece, that his son killed a man. Christ, I'm going to be locked up before I can wrap my head around this."

"You do believe me, don't you, Aunt Rogue?" She'd not known that Billy was in the house. Turning to her, she smiled and asked her to come and sit with them. "Mom is here. She wants to talk to Uncle Quin about the job."

"All right. We might as well share all of this. Did you tell her?" Billy nodded and smiled. "I take it she didn't think it was all that different."

"No. She said she'd been watching me with the neighbor's cats when we lived back home. Also with the animals here." Quin asked if she could speak to all animals. "Yes. All I've come across anyway. You should know that the mother cat in the barn is sick of hard cat food. She'd like something soft now that she's getting too old to have kitties."

Jane burst out laughing. It was as if all the tension of the room and the things being said were wiped out. Getting up, Rogue found the stash of cookies Mrs. Barclay had hidden from her husband and put them on the table. Not that she wanted to share the wonderful bits of sugary deliciousness, but this called for sweets and talk.

Rogue let everyone else do the talking. While she had about ten billion questions, they were being asked as soon as she thought of them. The one thing that bothered her the most, however, was what they were going to do about Robin. Something had to be done, or he was going to find out about Billy and hurt her. Worse, kill her.

The rest of the family showed up just as the cookies disappeared. Mrs. Barclay shooed them out of her domain, and they ended up in the living room, a room that Rogue was beginning to love most of all. However, now she understood the reason for four large couches. There were just too many large people in this family to make a normal three-piece set work. She looked at Quin when he said her name.

Are you all right with all this? I don't mean your niece, but with everyone being here? She smiled at him and told him through their link that she was slightly overwhelmed, but it had little to do with the crowd. *Yes, I'm right there with you. But this is a good thing. Without her, Robin might well have gotten away with a good deal more deaths.*

I'm just worried about what he'll try and do to her once he figures this out. I have no idea how he would connect the dots to her, but that's what is on my mind. He sat down next to her after shoving his brother Cass to the floor. Not that he seemed to mind. *I don't know why you thought sitting closer to me was going to make me less overwhelmed.*

It helps me. Now hush. I think we need to pay attention here. Parker has some news you need to know too. Parker turned and looked at her. There was still tension between the two of them, but they were working it out. *She's not going to hurt you.*

I know that, dumb ass. He laughed, and everyone turned to her. Embarrassed now, Rogue stood up and asked what was on her mind. How to keep her niece safe during all this. "I'd rather die than have anything happen to anyone in this family. Well, with the exception of Quin right now. But the rest of you, I can help out if you don't piss me off too much."

Laughter was just what she needed. As it seemed, the rest of them did. It was Parker that answered her. She might have said it earlier, but Rogue told the room she'd not been giving this her full attention. Rogue said she was still trying not to sound panicky when she thought of Robin.

"You don't have to worry about him killing anyone here. Not ever." Rogue asked why not. "You're immortal. Just the same as everyone in here is. Any of us can be hurt, and it will be painful, but nothing will kill us. You'll also heal a good deal faster than you would have as a human."

"But I am a human." Parker shook her head at her. "I am. I don't shift, fly, or do any of the things the rest of you can do."

"The moment you can Quin came together, that is when you changed. You have magic too. You can change your clothing at a moment's notice. Bring things to you that you might want. My favorite thing is this." She put her finger on the glass she was drinking from, and it filled. Not just with water, but also ice. "You'll need to drink more juice. Also, you'll have more magic once you and Quin bond. So get on that. It's important to your wellbeing."

The glass of clear water turned to a deep shade of red, like her favorite drink of raspberry tea. Drinking it down, it wasn't a surprise to see it refill. She looked over at Billy when she laughed. She apparently could do that as well. Billy's clothing changing was a little sickening, it was so fast. Rogue was happy to see that some of it was girly, but mostly things that would be nice to work in. She couldn't love these kids anymore if they were her own.

For the rest of the evening and well past dinner, they spoke about all the things that needed to happen before they could confront Robin or even his father. Rogue thought the best way was just as she did everything—straight to the point and telling Robby what they knew. Also, what Billy could do. It was thought that once she started working for the elderly man, he'd figure it out sooner or later anyway.

"I don't mind telling him. Just talking with you all has made me feel like I'm not some sort of a freak about this." Gabe, Lily's biological son, hugged Billy and told her it didn't matter about the animal talking stuff. She still was a freak. "Thanks, jerk."

Rogue loved that they never seemed to be at

odds with each other. While they did argue, it was never brought up how they weren't related, nor did Gabe point out that it was his mom and not theirs. It wasn't an issue. They all loved each other like they'd been born to the same parents.

It was about eight-thirty when someone came to the door. Not having a clue who it might have been, she wanted to hide away the kids and make sure she was armed. Instead of doing that, she sat with her hands under her legs and waited for the bad news to be dropped on them.

"Daddy?" Rogue looked to the doorway when Lily yelled. Getting up, not wanting to come between her dad and Lily, she hugged Lexi, her stepmother. "I'm so happy you came. I had no idea you were coming tonight."

After Lily moved back, Rogue hugged her dad. They'd been talking over the years, but this was so much better. Having Lily accepting Lexi and their dad's relationship with her made her heart extremely full. Then Lily introduced her children to their grandda.

"I'm a grandda again. I knew about Gabe, of course—Rogue told me—but I have a houseful. Oh my, come here and hug me. I've wanted to see all of you all my life." Sandy went right to her new grandda. After he picked her up and held her, she wiped the tears off his cheek, asking him if he was sorry about having grandkids. "Never, my dear child. Never. I've never been happier than I am right now about finding out that I have little ones to play with again."

Everyone introduced themselves to her dad. It was her that told them she and Quin were mates and that had dad sobbing again. Happy tears tore at her like sad ones did, and she joined her dad on the couch with a box of tissues between them.

"I want you to know, Mr. Fisher, that I'm going to let Rogue take very good care of me. Also, I don't think she'll allow me to be hurt either." Dad laughed and shook hands with Quin. After telling him to call him Roger, they settled down for a short but very needed talk. "You'll stay with us, of course. We have plenty of room and enough family around that you won't feel like a stranger at any time."

"I'd like that. If it's no trouble." Quin assured her dad that it wouldn't be. "Thank you, young man. You're just about what I expected for this one. A good man with a heart big enough to accept her challenges. She has a few too. I'll tell you about them sometime."

Showing her parents to their room, Quin held her hand as they walked to the living room again. Lily and her family went to their new home. The others had left just before her parents had been shown their rooms. Quin walked her to the living room and sat down on the floor in front of her. She was nervous about what he was going to tell her.

"Don't think the worst. All right?" She told him she'd try. "I'm in love with you. It's not been a gradual thing like I expected, but is hitting me right in my heart, so there was never going to be any room for anyone else. I know we have a long way to go in getting to know each other. But I would very much like for you to consider marrying me, for a lot of reasons. One of them is that I love you, but also because I need to know you're mine. Forever."

"Yes." He laughed and asked her what she meant. "Yes, I'll marry you. I love you as well. And like you, it was sort of like a slap in the face that I'm sitting in this big house with you and not enjoying all the benefits we could be sharing."

"Do you mean sleeping with me?" She asked him if he really thought there would be any sleeping going on. "No. Not much anyway. Christ, you have no idea how...well, maybe you do. I'll race you upstairs."

~*~

Quin wasn't mad. Not anymore. He was intrigued with what Rogue was doing at the crime scene she was working. While he didn't speak to her, he had a feeling she was getting more than she usually did as she stood over the bodies of three men with her camera pointed at them. Finally, when she looked at him, she asked the lead detective if she could have just a moment.

The phone call had come for Rogue almost as soon as they stepped into their bedroom. It was an emergency — in another state. She was to meet them in the back field in five minutes, or the police would come and get her. They opted for the chopper. Quin was happy when she said he was coming with her.

"Sure, Agent. You go right ahead. It's not like they're going anywhere." She glared at the younger man, and he shook his head and told her he was sorry. "I'm as sorry as I can be, ma'am. I'm new at this sort of scene and making jokes, however inappropriate, is my way of dealing with it. I swear I'll work on it from now on. I'm sorry. You go on ahead and take as long as you want. We'll wait for you."

She laid her camera on the table that had been set up for her. There were other pieces of equipment on the table — he recognized very little of it. When they were far enough away that he supposed they could talk, she put her head on his chest and spoke quietly.

"I can smell the person who did this. I don't know who it is, but I have a feeling I could find them if they were to walk past me. Not only that, but I can see things on the bodies that are giving me the willies." He asked her what she saw. "Fingerprints. I can see them as clearly as I can see you standing right here. Also, this is the worst. I can see not only how they were murdered but the order in which he cut them up and killed them. I'm not sure what to do with this,

Quin. It's really important stuff, but I can't just tell them it's new to me too, and this is what I can see."

"Take the pictures." She looked up at him. "Just take the pictures that you do and make observations as you go. Sort of like hinting, but more than that. Point out things you say you find on the camera lens, but it's really just you seeing it."

"I don't understand." Quin tried to think of a way to explain it to her without being more confusing. "Are you saying I should fudge it up? Tell them there are markings where I see prints, and I want them dusted? I can do that. Yeah, I can do that. Thanks." She kissed him and went back to work.

"Doctor Foster?" He turned and looked at the man standing not five feet from him. "I didn't mean to listen in, but I can help her too if she'll allow it."

"That'll be up to her, I'm thinking." The man, an Agent Carlson with the Feds, nodded. "You're a bear, correct?"

"Yes. Most of the people I work with are aware of it. Also that I can smell out things they normally wouldn't be able to. That's why I was assigned to Doctor Foster." He smiled. "I'm betting that gets confusing at your house. But she doesn't know. She might now, but she hadn't known that I was also here to protect her."

"I can't thank you enough for that. But as for you helping her, I can let her know you can do that.

I'm thinking she is a little nervous about giving away too much with this newfound magic. My brother is the king of lions, and she got more than her fair share once we found each other."

He didn't think it would be a good thing for him to say they also had a witch in the family. Parker was something that few believed in, and fewer still might be willing to think about being around her.

After telling Rogue about Carlson, he went into the room where the bodies were currently being photographed. Quin stayed out of their way and had a good look around where they were. It was in a town that might well have been abandoned before he was born. Not only that, it was deep in the woods around one of the biggest national parks in the United States.

I was wondering if I could come over and talk to Rogue for a little while. Her mind is blocked off from me. I wonder how she's doing that. He told Cass what she was doing and where they were. *I had no idea. Usually, I can hear overhead traffic when it flies over. Is she doing all right?*

She is, actually. Finding out a little more about her magic had her questioning herself for a minute, but she's back on track now. I can have her call you as soon as we're done here. She told me it usually takes about six to eight hours for her to be finished up. Something about the pictures loading up on the server takes a little longer. Cass told him that would be good but to wait till morning.

I forgot it was in the middle of the night. The moon is so bright here it's almost like daylight. I love it here.

I've not been there in ages. Yes, I can bet that without all the city smog, it is really nice there. Cass told him what he was looking to talk to Rogue about. *I told her we've served Missy with papers. The house and the bank account have been closed off to her too. I figured if she got wind of what we were doing, she'd make a hasty exit and perhaps take all the money and run. This way, I can keep her from doing that. Did you know Mark was worth a great deal of money? His insurance from his company alone is worth millions of dollars. They're the ones that are saying we should have his body exhumed and tested. Also, the coroner that I've spoken to about the body said he did blood tests on the man and woman that had been killed because he thought it was not just a run of the mill robbery at a convenience store. I'm not sure what he meant by that. I have a meeting with him tomorrow, but things are hinky if you ask me.*

Hinky? You've been hanging out with Grandma too much. But I understand. However, why exhume him? We all know he was murdered. What else could it be? Cass told him what he'd found out from the office he'd work out of. *So they think that up until his death, he was being poisoned? Again, why does it matter? Murdered is murdered, correct?*

Yes. But they seem to think it was his boss, a Mr. Charles Sampson, that might have been the one doing it.

Then when it seemed to be taking too long, he hired someone to take him out with a robbery. Cass also told him that if that was the case, there was more money coming to Lily and the kids. *Like millions more. Also, she'd own the shares that Sampson had, as well as her husband's. Oh, I did manage to find some money for Lily that Missy couldn't get to. The shares are worth a good deal, and the money from the stocks is going to be given to her in a fat check as soon as tomorrow from the dividends he had coming to him. He would normally reinvest his profits, but in this case, I thought it would help them along until I get this case won. I'm hoping I can be there when it comes. It'll be nice to see her win something wonderful for a change.*

So would I. I'm going to tell Rogue about this if you don't mind. I want her to be prepared for her sister when it gets there. Cass thought that was a good idea. *Thanks. I have them once in a while. By the way, the man Rogue works with is a bear shifter. He's been watching over her since she started working for them. Makes me feel better about her being gone when I can't go with her.*

I think it would me as well.

Cass told him he was going to bed, but he'd be up about eight. However, he wanted to have Rogue call him when she was finished working. Telling his brother he loved him and would see him tomorrow made him think he needed to tell them all that he loved them more often. He also decided he was going to tell his mom that too. Also, on the way back to his house, he was going to buy her some flowers. It had been a while since he'd gotten her any.

By two in the morning, Rogue declared herself finished. He had gone back into the building at one point and heard her talking to Carlson about the things she had noticed. Bruising here and there meant the victims had been touched by the murderer, so prints were taken in the area she suggested. Apparently, too, the camera she used was strong enough to pick up slight alterations in the skin when it came to things like that. He didn't have a clue but was glad it was helping the case move along.

Rogue decided to call Cass when she got up but did call him for a quick conversation. She told him she was exhausted, and he seemed to understand. But he did tell her about the money that would be coming to her house for Lily. She said she'd wait for him to show up before she called her over. After that, she fell asleep on Quin's shoulder for the rest of the ride home. Quin didn't bother waking her when they got there but picked her up and put her into their bed. They had the rest of their lives to make love, and he wasn't in any kind of hurry to do it. Well, he was, but he thought he could hold off for one more day.

Smiling to himself as he made his way down to the kitchen, he laughed when not only was Jude there enjoying a hearty breakfast, but his in-laws as well. Sitting with them, he figured he might as well get used to it. They were family, after all.

Getting his day started early was something he enjoyed more than getting started on time. Of course, he knew he was going to be exhausted when he was finished up for the day, but he was working on things he would need at his office at the horse ranch when Brook joined him. She was really getting large with child, so he made her have a seat before she could talk to him.

"I've only just realized that it's almost the end of summer." He nodded, with no idea where she might be going with this. "I'm getting there. Just hold your horses."

"I didn't say anything." She looked at him, and he was terrified she was going to start crying. He thought of a joke and told it to her. It was as lame as he thought it would have been, and she just stared at him. "I didn't want Ronan to come here and beat me up because I'd upset you."

"You didn't. I'm upset all the time now." He said it wouldn't matter to Ronan. "I've noticed that too. He's very...I was going to say weird, but that's not it either. It's almost like he's about to explode or something. I'm terrified to tell him I'm in labor. What do you think he'll do?"

"Explode. Just like you said." He thought about what she'd said. "What do you mean, you're terrified to tell him you're in labor? You mean when you go into labor, right?"

"No. I'm in labor now." He didn't move for nearly a full minute, then he made sure she was comfortable. Not that she was an animal, but he examined her and said she was as ready as she'd ever be. "Yeah, I thought so. As I said, I didn't want him to freak out. Will you tell him where I am and what's going on?"

"Sure, throw me under the bus." She laughed — having someone confirm she was in labor must have loosened her up a little because she laughed hard. "All right, but I want you to tell Rogue I love her very much, even though I had to more than likely deliver your baby while fending off the king of lions."

Telling Ronan was easier than he thought it would be. He didn't actually tell his brother but told his mom so she could tell him. When he showed up at his office with her, Quin was having Brook hold off on pushing so Ronan could be there when his child was born. As soon as he was ready, he had her bear down like she was having the greatest shit in the world.

"What a thing to say to someone." Rogue showed up with the bag that had been packed for Brook and the baby. Then she helped Ronan stay on his feet when his daughter made her entrance into the world. Christ, she was the most beautiful baby he'd ever delivered.

The second child was a little longer coming,

but when she came into the world screaming and crying, the entire room seemed to just break loose in cheers. He was an uncle again. And his brother was a dad. Nothing could have been better than to have a newborn, or in this case, newborns, bring everyone to a good mood. He certainly was now.

Since he wasn't a medical doctor, Brook made a call to her obstetrician. Once it was established that she was going to rest and be pampered, she okayed for Brook to recuperate at her own home in bed for the next couple of days. If the doctor had seen Brook while talking to her, she would have understood there wasn't any way she was going to rest, much less do it in a bed.

Taking the new family to their home, they had a small celebration with pizzas and cake.

"Do you want children?" Quin asked Rogue if she was asking him a trick question. "No. I'm serious. However, I can see where you'd think it was a joke. I want children. Not hundreds, but a couple. You?"

"As many as you will allow me to have with you." She rolled her eyes. "Now I'm being serious. It's your body, and I'd never do anything to make it so you weren't happy with me. If you only wanted one child with me, I'd be thrilled beyond words to see you large with our child. Or fifty. Which, I might point out, isn't a hundred."

"I'd like kids. Soon." He nodded, then wiggled

his brows at her. "Yes. I know how that works. We have to find time to actually make children to have them. My job, your job. Someday we might have to run away and have us a good fuck-fest without any interruptions. What do you think?"

"Fuck-fest? Yes, I'm all for a fuck-fest. When?" She said she'd have to make a couple of calls. "I will as well. I need to see if my insurance is paid up to date. You might not be able to kill me, but you can certainly make it so I'm incapacitated for a few years."

She was laughing as she walked away from him. Pulling out his phone, he called Robby to let him know what was going on. The man thought it was great that the two of them were getting away and offered them his home in Florida. Taking him up on the house, Quin made arrangements to fly there and have some fun. Robby was going to stock the place, whatever that meant to the older man. Not that it mattered. They'd be away, having fun, and no one would know where they were. At least until they came back.

Chapter 5

They flirted from the time they left the house to when they arrived at the airport. It had started out that her dad was going to keep an eye on the house for them, but in the end, they'd gotten Cass to do it. Rogue sort of hated to leave her dad when he'd only just arrived, but he told her that if he was given a house to use on the beach, he'd have left her too. Laughing, he also told her he and Lexi were going to move closer to her and Lily.

"I've missed a great deal, and I'd like to make up for lost time." She told him she thought them moving here would be a good start. "I've been talking to your sister a great deal too. She told me you had a long conversation with her."

"Not so long. But over the course of the years. She just needed to step back and look at the whole picture." Dad told her he was glad she'd done that.

"I didn't do it for you, Dad, but for her. I was afraid she'd get down the road, and it would be too late for her. She would be the one that carried the guilt. But I'm ever so happy the family is together again."

The check came just as they were leaving for the airport. Calling her sister and telling her to get her ass over to her house brought her over, but she was spitting mad when she got there, telling Rogue that she was in the middle of making her first batch of jelly when she'd called. All Rogue did was hand her the large envelope the courier had brought. When she glared at her several times as she tore it open, Rogue couldn't help but laugh at her.

"You're so going to regret looking at me like this when you see what is in there." Lily told her she doubted it. "All right. We'll see."

It was a good thing Quin had walked behind her when she pulled out the check. While she didn't know how much it was, Rogue did know it was more than a million dollars. The money hadn't been cashed in since Mark had died. When Lily was sat down on the chair, she asked her if this was a joke.

"You know me better than that. I'd never do anything so mean like that to you." Lily handed the check to her. After looking at it, she handed it back. "This should be enough to keep you going until the trial is over, I think."

"I should hope so. It's for seven million dollars.

Where the hell am I going to cash that size of a check? Do banks even have that much money?" She thought about it. "I wonder if I could have it all in ones. That way, I could have a nice bath in it."

"You'd have so many papercuts you'd so regret that. But seriously, you need to get with Cass. He's going to be the one getting this settled up for you and the kids. I'd talk to him about putting the money in a secure bank, one that Missy cannot touch." Rogue told Lily where the money had come from. "Mark took good care of you. So you could take good care of his children."

"They had to have my permission to have his body exhumed. I gave it, but then I was told it wasn't necessary. That someone had confessed to killing Mark. I was supposed to talk to Cass about it yesterday, but I got sidetracked with one of the kids." She told her what she knew. "Why would anyone kill him? Why would Sampson want to kill one of the nicest people there ever was?"

"Mark was planning to leave the company, as I'm sure you already knew." Lily told her he was going to be spending more time with her and the kids. They were going to have more. "I thought you would have known. But it was Mark's right to do so. He owned a part of the company too. Also, since he'd been there for so long, he wasn't under any kind of non-compete contract to make sure he didn't work for anyone in the same industry again. Sampson was afraid that once he started working on the same kind of programs his company was involved in, they'd find out that Mark was the only one that had done the work. The rest of them were hanging onto his success." Lily was crying a little as she explained to her about how he'd been slowly poisoning him. "Then when that didn't work as quickly as he'd hoped, Sampson hired someone to kill him. It just so happened that it was in a store where others were killed as well. Rather than face the death penalty, once the Feds told him about having the body exhumed, Sampson left a confession, then killed himself. You will be getting insurance money from that, as well as any and all shares that Sampson had."

"So much death. All Mark and I wanted to do was to have our own family and spend as much time as we could with them. We had made so many plans." Rogue hugged Lily and told her she'd be able to carry through on those plans for him. "I will too. I really will. Starting as soon as I figure out how to spend some of this money. What do you think of us going to an amusement park? With Lexi and Dad?"

"I think they would enjoy that more than they would anything else." They did have to move around their house sitter, but in the end, it worked out well for them all. Now here she and Quin were, on the plane to a destination she was excited to be going to with him and only him.

Almost as soon as they were in the lovely little house, it was like a home to them. There was enough food for them for the next few days, as well as fishing equipment and instructions on how to fish for their dinner. They would get to that, she was sure. But right now, all she wanted was Quin. Naked and in bed.

The room they were to use as their own was filled with flowers. Not only had Robby given them the house, but he'd made arrangements for them to have champagne, roses, as well as a huge basket of fresh fruits from around the area. Quin was having a piece of mango when she came out of the bathroom, undressed.

"You looked good enough to eat." She told him that was the idea. "Good. I have a hunger for you that I know will take me hours if not days to quench."

He moved toward her, tossing the last of the fruit over his shoulder and out the open window. Quin's body seemed to grow with each step. Not just his frame, but everything about him. Even his hunger, which she could feel, seemed to wrap around her until she didn't know where she ended and he began.

When he touched her with just the tips of his fingers, it was as if small electrical currents were set off under her skin. His mouth at her skin at the most sensitive parts of her body was overwhelming yet not enough, not nearly enough for her.

"Your skin is so soft. So warm." She couldn't speak. Her mouth was so dry. "I love the scent you're perfuming the air with. It's all yours. It makes me think of spring and the earth."

"Please, Quin. I'm so needy." He moved his hands, barely brushing her skin to her ass. It was enough to make her catch her breath. The way he cupped her had her crying out, the short climax, or whatever it was, taking her to highs she knew were only the beginning. "More. I need so much more. Please?"

He lifted her and fit her to his body. His cock, so thick, was pressed against her belly, and she reached down and ran her finger over the hard crown of him. When he cried out, his body bent back just enough from hers that she could take his hard nipple into her mouth. Rogue bit down on it hard enough to have him crying out her name. Begging her for more and telling her he couldn't take anything else, he pressed her against the wall behind her. Kissing her savagely, he pulled his mouth from hers just to watch her face as he adjusted her enough that he could slam his cock inside of her, filling her to the point where she was sure he was tearing her apart.

It took her a moment to realize he was talking to her. Then another moment to realize he was telling her how sorry he was. For what, she didn't know but wrapping her hands into his hair, she pulled him up to see into his face. Christ, what a wonderfully handsome and beautiful face he had too.

"Why are you sorry?" He said he'd hurt her. "A little, but that is to be expected, I think. You're built like a fucking horse."

His laughter made her smile. Standing with her back pressed against the wall, naked as the day she'd been born, with a man's cock deep inside her body, and he was laughing. She thought she should take offense but decided it was sort of charming.

"How did I live this long without you by my side?" Rogue told him he was just lucky. "No. I'm lucky now. Very much so. But if I don't move soon, I'm going to hurt myself and you too."

His body didn't so much move as it seemed to just slide in and out of her. Quin's hands never stopped moving, his mouth trailing quickly behind his finger. Every place his mouth nipped at her skin, he would kiss the tiny wounds he made. As she felt his movement, moving them to the bed, her body seemed to know to simply wrap around his. Her legs felt at home tightly around his hips. Her hands dug into his muscles as he did the same to her.

Her breasts were first abused, then loved. Each time her body felt like it was getting too much, he would touch her in another place where it wouldn't be enough. Rogue was sure he was trying his best to kill her with sex. Her body ached with each small climax that took her. Again and again, she thought for sure it was going to take her over the edge, take her to a place only reserved for people who were in love. And every time Quin would take her to the point, then pull back.

"If you don't let me come, I'm going to test the theory of how immortal you are." He laughed—it was almost too sexy for her when he suddenly took her deeper, his body seeming to plow her like she'd been needing for years...hell, her entire life. "More. Please, I want more."

He took her. There was no other way for her to describe how he not only brought her to the edge but followed her over until they were both hitting the ground at the same time and exploding.

Opening her eyes, she saw that at some point, he'd rolled to his back, and she was atop him. His soft snores didn't bother her so much as how he was holding her like he was afraid she was going to get away. Moving enough, so his hands dropped from her sides, Rogue rolled off Quin to the side of the bed to look at him.

Christ, he was hers, her mind and body thought. Her heart was so full she wasn't sure she could have had a single other thing touch it. As he turned and looked at her, his eyes the most beautiful shade of gold she'd ever seen, he took her hand to his mouth and kissed it.

"I'm broken." Rogue laughed. "That was far and away the most mind-blowing sex ever had by two people in the world. I don't think I can do that often. Unless, of course, you liked it so much you'd like me to do it every time. I'd suffer through it. Just for you."

"You're a goof." He rolled to his side, so he was facing her. "I'm starving. I mean, like I could eat a cow right now, and I'd not have enough."

"I know." He got up, his naked body covered in little bite marks she'd given him. Tiny bruises that were only just making an appearance. "I hope you like fruit. That's about all we have. Also, some of what appears to be chocolate cake in this thing. I'm not a big fan of chocolate, but I will share it with you."

They feasted on the things in the basket. In addition to the cake, which turned out to be white with chocolate frosting, there were small cans of sardines and crackers to eat them on. A roll of summer sausage and some dried fruits. Feeding one another each thing they found, the two of them sipped the champagne. It was the best meal she'd ever had, Rogue told Quin.

"I have to admit, I've never had better myself. But it's not going to be enough." He wiggled his brows at her. "However, I'm a little sore. How about we get dressed, go into town, and find us a sinfully expensive seafood place and have a nice dinner? Then walk around on the beach?"

"Heaven."

They ended up getting ice cream first, as their table was going to be a little while. The ice cream was hand-dipped, and they made pigs of themselves as they each ate a single cone. Dinner, too, was delicious. Even when she declared herself full, Rogue managed to eat dessert, having another dish of ice cream with bourbon poured over it and flamed.

The walk back to the beach house was with the two of them touching and talking about how much they loved one another. Before they were even in the house, Quin took her again, filling her up, making her scream several times as he pressed her against the front door.

Never had anyone made her feel this way. More than just loved, but also in love. Going to bed with him, they held each other tightly. Quin told her over and over how much he needed her, how much he loved her. Rogue said the same to him. She had no idea how she was going to return home. Return back to where she would have to deal with the life and death of her job. For the first time in her career, Rogue no longer wanted to work. She wanted to spend every waking moment with him.

~*~

They were enjoying the beach, lying in the sun, watching the shrimping boats pull in their catches when he turned to Rogue. He asked her about saving

Loman's life. She eyed him with one eye open and then turned back to looking out over the sea.

"I asked him about it. Twice. But he never told me. He said he wanted you to tell it. You would tell it the correct way." She snorted. "He also told me you shook the shit out of him to get him on the right track to keeping his grades up as well."

"He wasn't doing well in his classes. We shared a couple of them, and I'd watch him fuck off while he was in the room. The professors knew who he was and what he was, so they rarely bothered with telling him to drop the class if he wasn't going to work hard." Quin said that didn't sound like life or death. "It wasn't. Not then. But I'd had enough after…. One night, just after class, a bunch of us were walking back to the dorm. It had been a particularly brutal day, with most of us having second thoughts about what we were doing there. I saw a group of people running past us, but like I said, we were all pretty beaten up by class and didn't follow them."

He picked up several shells and laid them aside. Now that she was telling him, Quin wasn't so sure he wanted to know. Even finding out that Loman hadn't given college his best bothered him a great deal.

"There were five of them beating the shit out of Loman. Cass was there too, but he was already bleeding from a head wound and was unconscious. The men had tied them both up with silver chains.

That was my first clue that they knew the Foster brothers weren't human. The second one was that they made sure they were kept down so they'd not be able to shift and kill them." He told her they'd have not been able to shift without losing a paw or something worse. "I think I knew that on some level, but not at that time. I was terrified out of my mind for them. Don't get me wrong, I think Loman deserved what he got for fucking around in class, but this was more personal. It wasn't until later that I found out they thought Loman and Cass had raped one of the men's sister. Or something along those lines. Whatever they'd done, what they were having done to them was way out of line for anything other than murder. So, I stepped in and pulled out my gun. I was already carrying by then. It was a dangerous area I lived in at the time, and I wasn't going to die because some punk was armed, and I wasn't. So I shot one of the men."

The more he knew about her, the more he admired her. Rogue wasn't just a person out to make a living in the world, but she was trying her best to stay alive, make a difference, and make sure the underdog—his brothers, in this case—were safe, no matter how she felt about them.

"I thought they would scatter, but of course, you have stupid bravery when there is more than one dick in the bunch. So they fired back. I ended up killing two more of the men and injuring one, and then the one that was left tossed his guns down with the keys to the chains on your brothers and took off." He knew she'd been hurt too, but she skipped over that. That would be like her, he thought. Making things seem a lot less terrible than they really were. "Once I made sure they were both alive, I called the police and an ambulance. I don't think either of them had the strength to shift, but I wouldn't have allowed them to do it anyway. I had three dead men around us, and I wanted to prove I had to in order to save the two idiots."

They sat there for several minutes, neither of them saying anything as they watched the sun kiss the water on the other side of the ocean. The colors were such that he doubted even the best painter in the world would be able to capture them. They were there and gone so quickly. It was like a glimpse into something amazing. When it was just to the point where the darkness was about all they had, she spoke again.

"I don't think to this day they know how close they were to being killed. Loman might have known, but Cass doesn't. His head wound was deep enough that the doctor told me he could see his brain matter. Without him being able to shift for a few days, it was touch and go for him for a while." He asked about Loman. "He'd lost a great deal of blood. I mean, like more than even a shifter could stand to lose. I called in some favors and had some shifter buddies of mine give him a little of themselves. I didn't hate Loman. I want you to know that. He was a fuck off before this, and I didn't care for his actions. But I did know he had a family and that his mother would have been heartbroken if anything happened to him. She was all he talked about when he was screwing around in the classes. How she was the best cook in the world, and how much he missed being with her."

"Does Loman know about the other blood?" She said she'd told him while they were helping, but she wasn't sure he was up to hearing it. "What sort of blood? I'm grateful you did it and would ask you again to do so, but just for my own sake, what does he have to deal with someday? Like when his mate comes around."

"Vampire. Fae. I think Brook knows one of them. Jasper Shades." He nodded and smiled. "You think he'll be pissed off about that part? I don't care. I can take him on if need be, but I really don't want to lose a friend over saving his life."

"He won't be pissed off. And yes, Brook knows Jasper. We all do. Does Jasper know you're here? That you're my mate?" She asked him if he thought he'd care. "I don't know. But he is mated to Parker's sister. They have a set of twin boys. I think I'd mention it to him sometime to see what kind of things Loman might want to watch for. Anything else?"

"No. Mostly it was Jasper that helped. The vampire didn't want to get involved with a lion, so he only gave him just a little. Things weren't as soft and cuddly back then as they are now with vampires. They didn't like being put into a position where they might be beholden to someone, or vice-versa. Even I was a little leery of other shifters." He nodded and stood up. "Why did you ask about it? I don't mind telling you, but why did you ask me and not your brother?"

"He would have done the same thing you did when you told the story. Glossed over the parts where he was in it. I'm sure you were hurt. I'm also sure you were in the hospital for some time afterwards." She said it wasn't that bad. "No. I think it was really bad, and that the men who came to help you were there for you, and you asked them to help Cass and Loman. Correct?"

"So?" He laughed and pulled her up off the chair she'd been sitting in. "You're very handsome. And sexy. I don't think I tell you that often enough. I love you. Very much so."

"And I love you, my darling. Once we're home, we're going to figure out a schedule that allows us more time to do things like this. Getting away. Taking a break from stress." She said she'd love that. "Good. We'll make sure we do it then. Also, when the children come, I want to do this with them too. Not put off taking time for them because we have to work. I want them to enjoy being with us as much as we can."

"I'd love that. Making sure they know they're welcome on trips we take, even when business has to be a part of it. I don't mean just our children, but I'd very much like to include all the nieces and nephews too. I've missed Gabe growing up by working so much. I'd very much like to have them spending time with our kids too." He said he'd enjoy taking her dad and Lexi as well. "I think they'd have to get their own cabin or something."

"I have the money. I mean, to get us something to travel in if you wish." She frowned at him. "When my grandma first came here this time, she gave each of us an envelope to use for something fun. I've never spent mine. I have thought about it off and on since I met you, but now that we're talking about it, I think it would be so much more fun if we were to get us a big travel camper and live like heathens. I think they call it glamping. You know, glamorous camping kind of thing." She laughed and said she'd love that.

"I know a couple of people that camp. I think they have more fun with their kids being able to roam around in the big bus-looking thing than they do cooped up in the back of a car. Yes, let's do it. As soon as we get back. I think we still have time for a few trips before fall comes around." They were still talking about it when they went into town for dinner. He was enjoying the fresh seafood and told her that. "We can come here when we want. The Feds have a couple of dark houses—not safe houses, but dark houses—that other agents use when they need some time off like us. I think I'll put in for it a few times a year. Is that all right?"

"It's wonderful. I think we could even use it when we get to go onto my job. Quarter horses are in all kinds of races that we'd be able to go do. I haven't spoken to Robby about those, but I'm sure he'd like me to be there. This is getting more exciting all the time."

He was also liking the fact that they'd be together as a family when the kids came along. Or they adopted. In fact, when she pulled up the website of some campers near where they were, they decided to spend their last day there just looking for one they might like to use. He had a feeling they were going to be buying it and having it delivered to their home.

Not that he minded. His figuring was with all the dealerships around, they might even be able to get just what they wanted without having to order something. He knew they were going about this all wrong. Researching anything they'd need seemed to be something that neither of them wanted to invest any time in. But he thought that sometimes it was fun just to wing it. He didn't wing things very well usually. However, he thought this would be just the amount of fun the two of them needed.

By the time they were finished with dinner, they had a list of options they had decided they needed and things they didn't. According to the videos they'd watched, they knew storage was going to be something that, while it would seem as if there was plenty, it would never be enough. Especially when it came to having children in the home with them.

"You do realize we're going to have to get all kinds of things for the camper too?" He asked her what. "Well, linens. Also, we'll need to make sure we have all sorts of things to eat. Snacks and such. I love travelling and having snacks to eat."

"I did notice when we stop someplace you usually get something to eat. Even if we're headed to dinner." She kissed him on the mouth as she stepped into an ice cream shop. "See. Right there is what I'm talking about."

"Do you care?" He shook his head, telling her he loved her with all his heart. "And I need to keep up my strength so I can keep up with you. You're wearing me to the bones."

"You love that too." Christ, he loved this woman and didn't want to return to the real world. Just being with her over the last few days had been so nice he didn't want to return to reality. Not ever.

They were leaving the day after tomorrow.

Things were going to have to be put aside for a couple of days after getting there too. Neither of them had spoken about the list of shit that was going on, and he was all right with that. But soon, they'd have to deal with it. He just hoped it didn't take too much to settle up. Like the issues with Missy Tyler and Robin Quarter.

They would take care of those two things first, and he had a feeling the rest of it would simply fall into place. At least that's what he had hopes for. But with this family dynamics, who the hell knew what was going to happen daily? Laughing to himself, he took Rogue's hand into his as they walked along the boardwalk. For now, he just didn't care about anything but this woman.

Chapter 6

Robby didn't know what he could say to the young woman across from him. He'd thought of her as a child when he offered her the job. It was a lark on his part, but his mind was now working on all the things she'd told him. Also, some of the things he was almost too afraid to ask her about.

"Do you believe me?" He told Billy he did. He was just thinking. "Uncle Quin said you weren't a chatterbox and that you'd appreciate me not being one either. But I'm very nervous right now. Could you at least smile or something so I know you're not going to pull out a gun and kill me with it?"

"Good lord, child. I'd never do that. You've been honest with me. Honesty is always the best way to go. But this thing with my son? Well, it's going to take me a minute or two to think on it." He looked at her then, straight in the eye as she'd done with him when she'd spoken to him. "I think I knew he was screwing around with the horses and such. Not to the point you're telling me about, but that don't mean I'm not believing you. It's hard to...well, he's my son no matter what comes of this."

"Yes, sir." Billy looked over at her Aunt Rogue, a woman he'd come to admire more than he could remember ever thinking of a person he'd only just met. "This is a lot to give you at one time. I understand that. I only came here to tell you about the way I can talk to your horses. But you asked me what they'd told me, and I will never lie to you. I understand this might be something that will keep me from working for you—the knowledge that I'm not a normal kid. But I—"

"Listen, kid. There ain't a soul in this world that is normal. I don't know why that word even applies to anything anymore. Normal went out the window the day Adam was created. Nothing is just as it seems either. There are always things that will change, or even just tweak something, and it becomes the new normal." Robby laughed a little. "I like you, Billy. A great deal. You're smart, honest, and you have a good head on your shoulders. I like that in any person, male or female. And I want you to work for me, more now than before. You can tell me things I'd never get from that uncle of yours or even a man that has been training my horses as long as I've been selling them.

Things that will make me a better horse owner and a man who cares about the animals that put bread on my table. You remember this when you're out there and one of them people is telling you they're normal. They ain't, no more than you and me are. Now. I've had me a bit of thinking time, and I want you to tell me once again how you know about Robin and the pigs. Then I've got me some things I'll ask you about it, so I have my ducks all planted in the same row. All right?"

She told him, leaving out nothing at all this time. When he asked her a few things, she not only had the answers for him on most of them, but she was true to her word and told him honestly what she knew and what she didn't. There wasn't much of the latter, however.

"Now, these here pigs. Do you know what farm they're on?" She told him they were on his place. "I figured you were going to say that. I'll have to find them. Unless, of course, you have an idea where they are."

She not only knew but handed him a small piece of paper with the directions on how to get there. He didn't ask. Robby wanted to know who had given them to her, but he was afraid the answer was going to freak him out again. It never occurred to him how much more the animals knew about his farm than he knew. Like there not just being a pig farm on the land, but ponds he could be utilizing for the place too.

Something occurred to Robby as he was looking at the handwritten directions. Not that it hadn't occurred to him before, but now it wasn't just something that was a passing thought. He was in over his head when it came to his only child. Robin, for all his trouble, was even worse than he'd thought he was.

"I've messed up here. Not just with the horses. I can take care of them to the best of my ability, and I think I now have the best people on board to help out. But this thing with my son. I have a feeling I'm going to need more than just a little help on this." He looked at Rogue. "I know you offered, several times now, for you and your family to help me out with this, but I have only just realized I'm going to be messing it up because of what he is to me."

"No, I don't think you will, Robby. I think, and this could be just me listening to what you're saying, you've had an idea that your son was doing things you wouldn't have approved of for some time now. Billy here only gave you the proof." He said that was it. "We'll help you. We'll help you in any way you want. Or, and I think this might be best for you, we just go ahead and take over the problem and do it the way you'd want it done if he'd been anyone else."

"I'd have just shot him and been done with it." She didn't so much as blink at him when he said that.

Robby wasn't sure he didn't think this was just the way it should be handled. Robin was killing people and profiting from it and using Robby's ranch to do it from. "All right. I think I'd like you to take it over. I do want to know, but perhaps not until it's necessary that I do. I have it in my head that I'm also going to have to take some heat about this. I'll be all right with that so long as I know things are—"

"He's coming." No one moved when Billy spoke. The front door opened, and he could hear Robin bitching about the weather, which had turned out to be a rainy day instead of one of the nice sunny ones they'd had of late. Opening the door to his office, Robby watched as his son wiped his feet on the area rug in his room rather than outside, where the mud and dirt belonged. Robin didn't so much as look in the direction of the two women but told his dad about his morning so far.

"Robin, you're being rude. You should at least acknowledge the other people in the room. And next time you're thinking of coming into my office unannounced, I'd appreciate it if you were to knock." He asked him why he'd have to do that. "Because, as I pointed out to you before, it's not just rude, but what if I'd been having a meeting about something important? You would have been interrupting that."

"Dad, I hate to point it out to you, but you're old. And since we both know this place is going to need younger blood soon, you should be having me come and sit in on your meetings anyway." He glanced in the direction of Billy. "Don't get too comfy working here, kid. Once I own this place, you won't be anywhere near here. I have people that will do right by me, and I know you aren't really in need of a job in the first place. Your family has all the money."

"Robin Quarter." Robby was embarrassed by his son and the words coming out of his mouth. "You behave yourself. And I'm not so sure I'm leaving at all. Much less leaving this place to you. I kind of like working my own ranch."

"Whatever, Dad. No one lives forever. Now, as I was telling you about my morning, I'm going to need to borrow your company truck for a few days. I have some running around to do, and it involves toting things around that won't fit in my car." Robby asked him what sort of things. "Never you mind about that, Dad. I'm making progress on things, and sometimes it takes a little more than my little sports number to get those things taken care of."

"You mean the body you have hidden away? Or is it perhaps the money you stole off the car dealership you tore up two weeks ago? You remember the one, don't you, Robin? They allowed you to test drive a car even though you've had your license suspended for a year now. The man you beat up, he's going to press charges against you. I'm going to make sure of it." Robin looked at him, then turned in his chair and looked at Rogue. "There are all sorts of things I could tell you I know, but it would be easier for me to just tell you there is very little you do that I'm not aware of."

"You're full of shit." He looked at him. Robby looked hard at his son. That was when he noticed there was blood on his cheek. His hair also had small stains of it. Pointing these out of his son, Robin just laughed. "Dad, I'm not going to sit here and be accused of shit she knows nothing about. Just give me the fucking truck keys, and I'll be on my way. And for the way that I've been treated just now, I'd not expect to get them back anytime too soon."

"You didn't deny it." Robin asked him what he'd said. "I said you didn't deny it. The murder of a man. The car dealership. You didn't deny any of it. Nor did you seem too compelled in explaining why there is blood on your face."

"Dad, I don't know if you're aware of this or not, but I'm a grown fucking man, and I haven't had to explain myself to you in a very long time." Robby nodded but kept staring at his son, seeing him in a whole new light. Or perhaps, he thought, he was just now seeing him clearly. "This is ridiculous. I don't know where she got her information, but I'm telling you right now that I'm not going to sit here and try and explain myself to a stranger. Give me the keys, and I'll pretend like none of this happened."

"But I'm the one asking you." Robin stood up, and suddenly Robby was afraid. Not just that he'd hurt him, but that he would continue hurting others. "I'm not going to give you the keys so you can use my vehicle to cart a dead body out to the hog pen. Nor am I going to allow you to use my good name to get yourself out of things you've been doing. As of this moment, I'm going to do something I should have done years ago. I'm washing my hands of you."

"Because someone came here spouting things off that neither you nor they have any idea about." Robby stood up, straightening his body out its full length to let his son see he wasn't nearly as old or as feeble as Robin thought he might be. "Dad, you're making a mistake here. One that your ass can't cover."

"Am I? I don't think so. I think that not only can my ass cover what I'm going to say to you, but you're the one that will be in trouble." He didn't take his eyes off Robin as he spoke to Rogue. "Rogue, it's time you take over. If you'd be so kind as to call the police, I'd very much appreciate it. I'm going to give them whatever they want."

Robin drew back, and it was all Robby could do not to cringe from what he was sure would be a mighty blow. But he didn't hit him. Nor did his hand come forward in the least bit. It wasn't until he moved his head slightly that he could see that not only did

Rogue have this, but she had also put a gun to the back of Robin's head. As sure as he was standing there, he was positive she'd have no trouble at all in using it either.

"I've called the police, Mr. Quarter. They're on their way. And Aunt Parker is going to talk to them about where the bodies are that Robin has killed." Robin didn't move, but the hatred Robby could almost taste coming off his body was palpable. He thanked Billy. "You should also know that my family is on their way. Uncle Quin has been talking to them, and they're going to go out to the hog pen too. There is enough out there that they can figure out who has been put there by your son."

"You can't prove shit. This is going to be bad for you, Dad. You just wait and see." Robby told him he wasn't worried. "I'm not talking about the police, Dad, but what I'm going to do to you when I'm out of this shit. And there is no doubt at all that I'll be out before you can figure out where to hide from me. Because no matter where you go, I'm going to find you and kill your ass for this. The other two as well."

Suddenly he just dropped. There wasn't any kind of movement other than that Robin was suddenly on the floor. Robby looked at Rogue, who was smiling.

"Oops. I think I might have hit him too hard." Robby laughed. It was that, or he was going to cry.

"Robby, you have nothing to worry about from him. I swear to you that I will protect you as I would one of my family. Because you are to us. Family, I mean. He'll be in jail, then on to prison. Robin has a lot of things to answer for."

"I know." He did know, but it didn't make him feel any better that he'd let this slide by for so long. "I'm going to call my attorney and get things fixed up while he's gone. It's high time I started taking care of things the way I should have all along."

"Good for you." He looked at Billy when she spoke to him. "I want you to know something, Mr. Quarter. I was going to come out here and talk to you myself. You've made me feel that good about being able to come to you. I didn't feel like you'd have a problem with me being able to talk to the animals either. You, in just the few minutes I spoke to you before, made me feel like I was someone you could trust. And I trust you as well."

"Thank you, Billy. That was…well, honey, that was just what I needed, I think." She nodded, then did something he thought she rarely did — she hugged him. Tightly too. It was then that Robby realized it had been much too long since anyone had hugged him. It was something else he was going to change. He was going to be a more approachable man from now on. "You come on back out whenever you can, child. I'd like to talk to you about some other things.

Do you play chess?"

"Yes. My dad taught me." He nodded. "I'm going to be happy to work for you too. And I'll feel safer. Thank you, sir, for the opportunity to do what I've wanted to do all my life. Work with horses."

Going to his office after Robin was taken away and the women left, he called his attorney. It was something he'd been meaning to do for some time now. Charlie had been telling him it was time to update for years.

"Christ, I'm so happy to hear that. I was just thinking about you the other day and how I needed to call you." He told Charlie what had happened and what was going on. "You're going to need an attorney too, Robby. I'll see what I can find out for you on my end. If you say the Fosters are working with you, I'll rest easier knowing you're in good hands. Is Cass going to represent you?"

"I never thought to ask, but I will. You won't do it?" He said he wasn't up to date on laws concerning what he'd need, but he knew Cass was the best. "Then I'll see. They told me they'd take care that I was taken care of. An old man like me sure does like it when people say that to him rather than threatening him about how they're going to kill him. I tell you, Charlie, I've never been so afraid in my life until then."

"I can understand that. I certainly can. But you ask, and I'll wait to hear from you. Also, since I'm assuming you're not leaving him the ranch, you're going to have to think of someone or something to do with it." He said he'd think on it, but he had a good idea. "I'm sure you do. And so you know, I'm going to change over your other policies as well. Some of them still have your wife's name on them as beneficiary. That is something else we'll need to take care of. I'll take care of the banking information now. I don't want anyone coming in to say you have to cover anything Robin has done. He's what, in his thirties now?"

He had to think and realized his son was coming up on his fortieth soon. "Yes, I think this is good timing. Taking him out of the will, that'll have to be first and foremost. Changing the locks is another thing I'll have done before I see you."

Charlie said he'd see him tomorrow and that he'd have everything but the beneficiary taken care of. After talking to him for a little bit longer, he called Cass. Might as well figure out if he had the best wording in the will so Robin couldn't get a damned thing. Cass wasn't in, but he was able to leave a message. After that, Robby decided he wanted a thick steak for dinner. Calling up Quin, he had him meet him in town. It was time to get things rolling in a much better direction.

~*~

Missy wasn't sure what all the hoopla was about, but the courtroom was packed. She'd been brought here by the police last night when she'd been arrested. It had taken her most of the day to have someone notice she was shoplifting. Starved and without a place to stay, she'd had to resort to other means of getting something in her belly and clean clothing. She was going to bring that up at this hearing as well.

They'd been kind enough to feed her, even though it was past dinner time. The officers had also offered her a much-needed shower, as well as an extra bar of soap so she could scrub her underthings. Missy couldn't remember being this broke before. Not that she was really broke, but having no access to her funds was putting a huge damper on her days. That was on her list too.

When the courtroom was called to order, she waited until she was asked if she had anything to say before she nodded, standing up. Missy had seen enough court dramas to know that misbehaving wouldn't get her shit. It was the polite and intelligent people that got off. She was good at that. Not only that, but she thought of herself as smart enough to know when to shut up and when to speak. Today was going to be testing the limits of her ability to do the first part.

"Ms. Tyler, I'm to understand from your court-appointed attorney that you've decided to represent yourself in this. Do you believe that's a good move?"

She said she was sure it was. "All right then. We'll begin. It says here that you've bribed a sitting judge, committed insurance fraud, as well as theft of a house." He looked at her. "How does one go about stealing a house?"

"She was stupid, I guess. And that is why I don't think I should have any of this held against me, Your Honor. What sane person thinks an ex-wife would have any rights to anything her ex-husband left specific instructions to give to his current girlfriend? I know, I know what you're going to say. It was still stealing from her. Well, she didn't have enough sense to fight very hard for it, so my thinking is, she doesn't deserve anything. I should just be able to go on as I have been." Missy laughed. "Then there are the children. She actually took on three brats that didn't belong to her. And if that wasn't enough, she didn't even fight me for any kind of support since they're my kids. See? Stupid on all accounts."

"So you're admitting to fraud? You're telling me you knew you were entitled to none of the things you've taken from Ms. Fisher, and you still did it?" Missy was sensing that the man wasn't understanding the totality of the situation, and she explained it to him again. "I understand that you believe Ms. Fisher to be stupid. You've pointed your opinion out on that matter several times. However, you've not explained to me why you bribed a judge and committed all kinds of fraudulent acts against this young woman, not to mention your own children."

"I don't know why I'd have to explain this to you either, but I was out for a little fun. It's not at all my fault that she didn't have the funds to make sure that she won, and I didn't." There were people in the room acting like they'd never heard of the concept of trying something out for the fun of it. "Look. Everyone likes to shake things up a little. Fun is what makes us young and happy. Don't you see? I don't know what to tell you, Your Honor. I've been enjoying living in the lap of luxury. Being able to come and go as I please without a worry one. There this woman sits with too many children and no money." When the attorney sitting next to Lily stood up, clearing his throat, she turned to him. "I don't know what you think you're going to gain by interrupting the big boys here, but say your piece, then sit down and shut up. We're talking here, and whatever input you have to say on this is a moot point."

"Thank you ever so much for your permission to speak." The man handed the paperwork to the judge, who looked it over then handed it back. When she was handed the same paperwork, she just laid it aside. It was meaningless to her anyway. "You might want to take a look at that, Ms. Tyler. It might well be your downfall."

"Doubtful. I'm not nearly as stupid as your

client is." She didn't even bother with looking even when he walked away. "What do you say, Judge? Am I going to have to pull out my wallet for you as well? I can tell you right now you're going to have to hold the check for a couple of days. At least until you get them to take the hold off my accounts and credit cards."

She smiled when he cocked a brow at her. Missy wasn't worried. Whatever happened after this, she'd be home in time for dinner after taking a much-needed shower then soaking in the tub.

The man that had interrupted her stood up again. "Your Honor, this is a blatant crime of Ms. Tyler's to not only get rid of her children but to also take the safety and security of their livelihood from them. Not only that, but she attempted to bribe you in open court if that was what it would take for you to see things her way." She turned to him, not remembering his name, but he put up his hand. "You shut your trap, Ms. Tyler. I've had about enough of you and your badgering and bullying today. What you did is horrendous. Not only to Ms. Fisher but to your children that she's been taking care of since her future husband was murdered."

"She seems to be doing all right." Missy turned back to the judge. "So, what's it going to be? Do I pay you as I did the other guy, or are we just going to call it a day and I get my things back? Either way is fine by me. I just want this over with. And also, can you make it some kind of rule that she can't do this every few years? It's ridiculous to have me locked out of my home and having my life disrupted again and again."

"Oh, I think we can call it a day." She was happy. It wasn't going to cost her an arm and a leg to get this thing done and over with. "And I think I can assure that Ms. Fisher won't have to come back to you for the money and property anymore. Melissa Tyler, I find you guilty on all counts brought before me today. Since you have willingly and without any encouragement simply told us all that you're not above bribing me or anyone else that will get things moving for you, I find no reason to waste the taxpayers' money on what I would think would be a short trial. You will be taken to federal prison upon leaving here, and—"

"Wait. That's not going to work. I have to get home and take a bath." He looked at her oddly again. "Seriously. Just let me write you out a check, and we'll call it even. All right?"

"Bailiff, I want her out of my courtroom now. I cannot stand to hear her voice anymore." Missy told him he was making a huge mistake. "And why is that?"

"I'm not going to go away quietly. I know people." The judge asked her what sort of people she might know. "The kind that will take you to task if you don't listen to what I'm telling you to do."

"Did you just threaten me?" She just stared at him, knowing he'd get it sooner or later. "Get her out of here now."

Missy thought things did end up well until she was put back into the van she'd come here in. Telling the person locking her into the seat that the judge had let her go, no one would answer her about when she was going to get to go home. People needed to realize this wasn't the way things went. When she told them she'd pay, she would. Didn't they realize how much she was worth? Apparently, she was going to have to have a talk with someone about this. They'd have to get her out of this mess, or she'd have to take action.

Missy sat back in her seat and waited. She tried to tell herself they were just running her by the jail to get something, but she had a feeling she wasn't going anywhere just yet. Whatever happened in the next few hours, someone was going to pay. And it wasn't going to be her. Missy wasn't stupid like the cow Lily was. She needed to get her things in order and take her to court once again. It wasn't that she thought she was above the law, but if there was money, that should count for something. Missy wasn't going to be pissy, but this really was going to make her have to hold onto her temper a little tighter for a few hours, then all bets were off. She was going to have to make some serious promises with money. People were starting to get on her nerves just a little too much.

"Ms. Tyler?" She nodded, asking the guard if she was going to get to talk to the judge again. "No. He's made his decision. I have a list here that I'm to read to you if you'd like. Or I can give it to you. So you know, it's going to be recorded that I read it or handed it over to you."

"What sort of list?" The guard nodded and pulled open the envelope. "Just give it to me. You'll be stumbling over words, and we'll be all day."

Once she was handed the envelope, the woman just stood there. Asking her what she was doing now, she said she had to stay to see if Missy had any comments after reading it. Pissed off, she started reading the list, as it was called.

"This says I'm to give up the money, the cars, houses, and property that now belong to Lily. That's not what we agreed on." She asked her if the judge had said those words. "Well, no. But I was going to give him a kickback for helping me get the things back to the way I wanted them."

"Apparently, he can't be bought."

The guard walked away. No matter how many times Missy called for her to return, she didn't. Picking up the paperwork again, she read on. There were other things she was going to be giving to the cow, like her own bank account money and any and all homes she might own. But—and this was the real kicker—she was still going to be paying on the unpaid bills she'd accumulated while enjoying—it actually said enjoying—her time in prison.

Missy sat there thinking about what had happened. It occurred to her that she was in deeper shit than she'd ever been. Not only that, but she was also going to prison, and it seemed there was very little to nothing she could do about it.

"Maybe she was a little smarter than I was." She'd never say that to the other woman, but she knew it to be true. "I've been royally fucked, it seems."

Chapter 7

"That takes care of the newspaper articles that Missy took out slamming Rogue on her work. With that, along with a retraction from Missy's attorney on all the trouble caused by her bribing the judge, the bill collectors you had before are being taken care of. You need to decide what you want to do with the house you shared with Mark, along with the accounts he has concerning the business. As Cass said, you can hire someone to take care of that if you wish." Quin glanced at Rogue. Lily was still looking poleaxed, which he didn't blame her for, but she needed to be shaken out of it before she had to make an appearance before the judge. "The money you wanted to be set up in your children's names has been finalized as of this morning."

"Lily, what's the matter?" She looked at her sister, then at him. He had a feeling she'd not only not been paying attention to him but that she'd not been paying attention since she'd arrived a couple of hours ago. "Lily, we've been talking about your money and what needs to be done now."

"I know I have a lot of it. Millions and millions. But right now, I'm having trouble getting around the fact that Missy thought I was stupid." Rogue snorted. "Well, she said it several times to me. I think that wasn't anything I missed."

"No, you didn't miss anything. However, what you are missing is the fact that you're not in jail and that woman is." This time Lily snorted. "I don't think I've ever heard you do that before. Are you perhaps taking on a new life?"

"No. I'm thinking that is the stupidest thing you've ever said to me. She's in jail, and I'm not. She should have been there from the very beginning."

Quin leaned back in his chair and watched the two of them. He'd seen them fighting before. It was epic how they would resort to name-calling, then hug and sob, telling each other how sorry they were. He and his brothers would fight with fists and teeth. These two were so civilized it was almost boring to watch.

"What the hell am I supposed to do with all this money?" Lily continued. "Not to mention, I think I was told I have three houses, as well as a boat someplace, and some kind of winter home. What the hell is a winter home? And why on earth would someone want to go to a house in the winter months when it's flipping cold?"

"First of all, you have a boat in Florida. I told you that." Lily growled, and Quin had to hold his laughter. "Secondly, you have a winter home, *where it is warmer than here,* and you go stay so you can keep up with your tan."

"I don't tan, and you well know it." Rogue said she was missing the point. "No. I'm not. I'm flipping overwhelmed, and I—"

"*Fucking.* Say it, Lily. You're fucking overwhelmed, and it's getting to you. You might feel a good deal better if you were to say the word once in a while. Or better yet, get fucked. Getting laid might loosen you up a little bit."

Quin left the two of them before they turned their anger on him. Not that he would have minded so much Rogue being upset with him. But Lily would sob how sorry she was and hug and hold him, and she'd felt terrible. He would end up feeling worse than she did, and he'd only been an innocent bystander.

"I was just going to go and talk to you, but I heard the girls in there talking." Roger asked him if he had a few minutes. "I have some things I'd like to talk to you about. None of it is earth-shattering, but I do need to talk to you."

"Absolutely. Anytime, you know that." Roger

nodded. "I'm betting it has a little to do with the money that was put into your account this morning. I want you to know that had it been me, I'd have maxed out the account and given you access to more should you have needed it."

"I don't need what is in there now." Offering Roger a glass of tea, he poured himself some as well. "That's a great deal of money. And while I'm aware that my daughters are wealthy, that doesn't mean they had to share with me."

"Yes, it does." Roger asked him why. "Lots of reasons come to mind, but I'll tell you the one that Lily and Rogue said to me. You're going to be living for a very long time, and neither one of them wants you to ever be unable to take the children anywhere you want because of lack of funds or lack of time. This way, you can go and come with them as you please and not have to work around a schedule that might hold you back from enjoying them."

"Still, that's a great deal of scheduling." Quin asked him if he'd had a good time at the park with them. He didn't really need to answer him. It was written all over his face. "Oh, you have no idea. It was like a dream come true for me. I didn't worry about money. I didn't worry about the food we ate. It was such a wonderful trip that next year, I'm going to purchase a membership." Roger sat there for a few seconds. "I get it now. I mean, just like that, it was as clear as day what you were telling me. Thanks."

"My pleasure. But I'm glad I can talk to you. I wanted to ask you about your housing. I would love for you two to live here for the rest of your lives, but I do understand that you'd like some space of your own. I think you also mentioned you'd like to put in a little garden, as well as have enough room for your grandkids to come and stay with you." He said the bedrooms were a must, but the garden was open. "I'm glad to hear that. There is a large piece of property at the end of my mother's land that she would like to gift to you. She said she's going to give it to you anyway, so you might as well take it."

Quin handed him the envelope with the deed in it already turned over in Roger and Lexi's name. When Roger read it over, he laid it down and started crying. Quin was all right in handling the tears of women, but men, not so much. He waited until the older man was able to regain control of himself.

"I don't know what to say." He told him to say thank you and move on. "Your mother, your entire family, has been a Godsend to my family. If not for you and yours, I don't know where I'd be right now. Certainly not being able to visit with my daughters and grandchildren."

"I'm glad to hear you say that. I thought for sure I was going to have to call my mom here and have her knock you around a little." Roger laughed, saying he thought she'd do more than that. "You should also know that there are workers ready to start on the house as soon as you wish. There is no hurry, of course, but I wanted to let you know that."

"Thank you. That seems so lame, but I sincerely mean it." They talked about the house, as well as anything else that came to their minds. He liked Roger. Lexi too. They were a good couple, and they were having a great deal of fun being around all the kids. "The other day, Gabe asked Lexi if he could call her Grandma. I thought she was going to cry for a week. But after that, they all started calling both of us grandparents. I have to tell you, there is no sweeter word than being called that. I never thought it would happen for me."

"You're a lucky man, Roger. We both are." When the women joined them in the kitchen, Lexi was with them. They'd been crying again, and he could only hope they got over this soon. It tore at his heart when they did that. "Roger and I were just talking about dinner plans. Do you ladies have any? Because we were thinking we'd like to take the most beautiful women in this house out."

"Good save." He grinned at Rogue. "We were just talking about that as well. While having dinner with you guys seems like a fun night, we were thinking it's been a while since all of us hit up a restaurant. I've already contacted the rest of the family, and they're going to meet us there at six. Even your mom is going to cut out early from the barn she's been working with and meet us there."

"I forgot they were putting up walls today. Brook said she'd been able to save a great deal of the wood, as well as some of the bricks that were used around it. I can't wait until it's ready to use." Rogue told him it was supposed to be done by the fall. "I wonder if Mom would like to have something for the grand opening, like perhaps a huge Thanksgiving feast, and invite the townspeople."

They talked about that all the way through the time to leave. Even on the way to the place, he and Rogue spoke about the things that had been found in the foundation, as well as how it had been a hoot to have seen the old bathrooms that had been in the thing. As they were pulling into the parking lot, he could see where the building was being worked on, and since they were early, they headed in that direction.

Not only were the walls all up but the inside of it was nearly finished being drywalled. They were leaving enough of the posts up, so it retained its natural look. But as Mom had wanted to be able to use it year-round, the walls had been insulated, and not just a furnace, but air had been put in as well. The large kitchen was nearly finished except for the stock being put on the shelves, and Quin loved that there were enough ovens and stovetops that even an army could be fed in there.

"There is going to be a gaming room too. Not for adults, but for kids. There will be beds and a fridge put in for the little ones." His mom joined him in the room and showed them around what was going in and what yet had to be installed. "I've never had so much fun spending money for a good cause in my life."

"It looks done for the most part. I can't believe how much you've gotten done in a month." Neither did his mom, apparently. "I guess when you have money, as you said, it's nice to be able to spread it around a little."

"The pool is going to surprise everyone, I think. Of course, it won't be filled up this year, but next year it will be a nice place for families to hang out. There is going to be a snack bar too." Mom thanked Rogue for suggesting it. "The idea came in that kids should be able to work in the place in the summer months for a tab when they come here. I love that it's going to be a community thing."

Mom wasn't keen on charging people for the pool, but Cass pointed out that insurance and maintenance were going to be expensive. He also said if they charged even a little, it would be more of a treat than just something to do when they wanted to come over. Quin could tell she was still on the fence about it, but he knew Cas was right. There was no point in making things too easy on the town.

Quin spoke to his mom about Thanksgiving, and she was all for it. Her suggestion was that they cooked all the food and let each family bring their own place setting. It would save them on washing everything to be put away again. Even though there were two dishwashers in the kitchen, having people bring their own plates would keep down the cost of that as well.

"I'd suggest a sign-up sheet too. Not just for those who are coming, but for some people to come in and help cook, as well as cut up the food for this. It might go better that way where you're not worn out from cooking about fifty turkeys while the other people are home relaxing." Mom told him that was a great idea. "I would also like to suggest that we hire some of the kids at the school to help out. Cleaning up or even getting coffee and other drinks. I'd be willing to pay them if they wanted to use the money for band or whatever club they might be in."

"Yes, that's wonderful. I know that sometime in March, the band has already set up a time to use the building for a large garage sale. They're renting tables for people to use. Also, they're taking donations of items they can sell themselves. I know Ronan and Brook have said they'd supply the food for them to sell. Oh, this is going to be so good for the town, son. I cannot wait for it to be finished so we can get things moving in it."

Quin hugged his mom as they were being seated.

The others were already seated and had drinks. Instead of giving them a hard time about being late, they asked about the barn and what kind of things had been done. Brook said she thought it was not only going to come in under budget, but it might be ready as much as ten days earlier than she'd said. Not that there had been a budget to work with. Brook and her crew weren't charging his mom anything for the work or the material.

Dinner was fun, loud, and friendly. With their ever-growing family, he was sure they were going to have to rent an entire restaurant when the time came to do this in the future. Perhaps they'd use the barn. Quin knew for a fact there were several large smokers and grills being put together for anyone to use. It might be more fun to do it that way, he thought, rather than having to watch themselves with how loud they were, and they could be themselves more. Quin thought it might be fun to even be able to shift for the kids once in a while. He thought both the human and shifter kids would have fun with that.

"I wanted to talk to you about something." Ronan sat down next to him after their plates had been taken away. "There is some talk about town that there are two industries coming in. Have you heard anything?"

"No, but then I've been out of town for the last few days." He said he'd seen his travel home. "Thanks. We're planning our first trip in a few weeks. What kind of industries have you heard about?"

"One of them is a place that makes boxes. Custom ones that will have names on them. The other I've not been able to find out about. No one in the family has any knowledge of it either." Quin told him it was probably that, just a rumor. "That's what I was thinking too. Just something that would get people excited, only to disappoint them. Cass told me that you and he were going to go with Robby to talk to his son. I guess I never knew some of the things he's been doing."

"Me either, to be honest with you. If not for Billy, I'm not sure how much longer it would have been going on." They talked about the young girl and her abilities. "She told me some things I think you should be aware of, especially before the next meeting. There are some rumors going around that you and Brook might have a little bit of an issue. Something about the new rules that have been put in place. I might have been aware there are new ones, but I won't lie to you and tell you I've read them to any extent."

"They're replacement rules for some of the more archaic ones that were in place, like women being able to drive a car. I know it's not been enforced for a long time, but I took it out so I could put in one about women being able to have a full-time job. Also, the byline that I put on it says that if the mate isn't working, and it isn't due to any good medical reason, such as he's ill or incapacitated in some way medically, he can't just assume the money his wife earns is for him. Also, it doesn't count if one of them is going to college for the betterment of the family, so long as they both agree to it. However, he isn't entitled to have access to the funds before bills and family needs are met. I'm betting that is the one people don't care for."

"I love that one. Can you imagine how much better Mom's life would have been had Dad not been able to just take out money when it was there?" Ronan said that was the main reason for the new rule. "Good for you. The one I've been hearing the most buzz about is the banking rules. The one where it says all pride members must go through the local banks when they are in need of funding. That'll help the entire town out."

"Thanks, but I don't know how much of that one I'm going to be able to enforce. There was a rule in there that said the pride leader—that would be me—would loan money to any pride member that couldn't secure a loan. Also, that I would never be able to ask that they repay it if times were hard. That one had to go. I can imagine having people lined up out the door for that one had it still been in there. Lucky for me, we found it before I had every pride member sign off that they'd read all the rules." Quin laughed and asked him if he was sure he'd gotten it out in time. "I'm sure. I had Brook go over it three times, and then Mom before I had copies of it made. There are still some in there that might have to be taken out sooner or later, but for now, I can live with the ones we have."

"I'll get on to reading my copy as soon as I can." Ronan thanked him. "Roger and Lexi are going to stick around. I'm still wondering what Lily is going to do. She's so stressed out about having all this money it's hard for her to focus on much of anything else. But I did go over it with her, and I'm thinking Rogue will as well. She'll slap her around a little and get her to make a decision. The house is the most important thing. It can't sit empty for too long. I'd hate to think someone like Missy would move in."

"She's left for the big house, I heard." Quin said he'd heard that as well. "Then there is Robin. I never liked that man even as a kid. He was forever having something or someone doing shit for him. Lucky for us, we were always bigger than him. And us being cats kept him away from us. Mom told me she'd babysat him once and never again. He was a terror even back then."

Quin wasn't looking forward to going with Robby tomorrow, but he'd told him he'd be there for him. Robin was going to have a long trial, and it was going to be an eye-opener for a lot of people. He'd been dealing in death for a long time. Lucky for everyone involved, Billy had been able to talk to the animals involved and had found a lot of evidence that would be used against the man. Good. The streets would be so much better without him walking around free.

~*~

Rogue was sitting in for Quin today as he'd been called away for an emergency. She'd been happy to be there for Robby. She also wanted to hear firsthand what the hell the man, Robin, had to say for himself. She also knew that Robby had a few things to say to his son, one of them being that he was washing his hands of him forever. Rogue didn't think Robin would say much to that, but it was going to be put out there so Robby wouldn't be saddled with Robin's shit.

When he joined them in the large conference room, Robin was sporting not just a black eye but what appeared to be about ten stitches in his lower lip. Instead of commenting on it, Cass told Robin they were recording this conversation. Robin was also informed he would be given a copy of it once it was transcribed.

"Why would I need that? You think I might come back on you, Dad? I don't care what you have to say to me today. I know what I know." Robby asked him what he thought he knew. "That you're going to get up off your high horse and get me the hell out of here. Whatever burr you have up your ass about things is going to get you into a serious lot of trouble."

"Really? From where I'm sitting, Robin, I'd say it's a safe bet that you can't do anything to me. Not unless you break out of jail and come after me. But that's not going to happen either. Not where they're sending you. You've hit the big time, Robin. They're sending you to the worst prison in the world. And no one ever comes out of there unless it's in a body bag." Robin snorted, and Rogue decided right then and there she was finished with that sound. "I've come here today to inform you of a few changes I've made. All of them are concerning you and your being my only son."

"You might want to keep reminding yourself of that, Father dearest. I'm the only person you have left in the world right now." Robby smiled, and Rogue thought it was a very good smile. "What? Are you going to tell me you're taking me out of the will? You can't do that either. It's my right as your son to inherit your stuff."

"No, it's my right to refuse you anything. As of yesterday morning, a new will was written up and filed, so there are no more issues with what I have and what I leave to whoever I wish. You are no longer mentioned in it, other than to say that you are entitled to nothing." Robin said he was a liar. "If you say so."

Robin looked at Rogue. "I suppose you have a lot to do with this. Some dyke that orders my father around—"

The chair Robin was sitting in just fell back. If not for the fact that Robin was chained to the table, he might well have tipped all the way back. Rogue looked at Cass when he sat back down after hitting Robin.

"There will be no more talk like that. Now, here is a copy of the will for your reading pleasure. You'll note that, as you were told, you are not mentioned in the will as anyone that would need to be showing up for things given over to you. You are getting nothing."

Cass went on to talk about who was mentioned in the will, and it occurred to her that Billy had been mentioned. Before she could ask what that meant, Robin asked.

"Billy has been a better friend and daughter to me than you ever were a son. So, as for her name being mentioned, you'll see right there that I'm leaving a little something for her to live on should she want it. The horses, the estate, and any money in the bank when I kick the bucket, she'll get a part of. Which I'm thinking will be long after you're dust in the ground. By the way, you're not going to be buried on my land either. You've done enough to it to last several lifetimes." Robin said he wasn't being fair. "Fair or not, that's the way I've decided to do it."

When Robby stood up, she did as well. Cass told them he had some things he needed to go over with Robin before he left, and they were to meet him in the cafeteria. She and Robby were about halfway there when the older man broke down. She knew he was having a hard time with this, and she was hurting for him.

"He actually said it wasn't fair. Like him killing off people was fair to them." She stood there while he blew his nose and sniffled. "I should be used to his crap by now, but I tell you, it just makes me happy his mother isn't here to see him like this. She'd be more hurt than I am."

"He's lucky Cass hit him before I did." Robby laughed and hugged her. "How about we go and have us some pie? I think pie cures everything going wrong. If they were to have a meeting between two opposing countries, serving them pie would be just the ticket."

"I think you might be right on that one." He moved along the hallway with her and stopped when he laughed. "Perhaps that's what happened to Robin. He told me when he was little that he just couldn't stand pie. I guess I know why now. Damned kid. Who doesn't like pie?"

They were still laughing when they picked out their dessert. They each had four pieces, and the plan was to taste them all. Just a taste. But in the end, they ate each slice and enjoyed every sinful bite. When Cass joined them, he didn't have much to say that was good, she supposed, but he did look upset for a while. Then Robby bought him some pie, and he looked better.

Perhaps she was right. Pie did make things better.

Chapter 8

Cass sat down next to the man he'd come to respect a great deal over the last few days. Robby Quarter was not only a good man, but he was very troubled. The word had come to him that there was a child out there that belonged to Robin, and Robby had jumped at the chance to go see the child and mother. Not that they had DNA proof it was his child, they did have a whereabouts for it that the two of them had followed to where they were now.

"I've spoken to the principal of the school the child might be attending, and she told me if it's who she thinks it is, they're in financial trouble. Also, if this is Robin's, there are twin boys, not a single child as we were looking for." Robby looked at him with so much hope in his eyes that it hurt Cass to have to tell him the next part. "The woman, their mother, is working several jobs and sleeps while they're at school. I have, with my own money, deposited two hundred dollars. Even if she's not who we think she might be, I have to help her out. She really is in trouble."

"I'll pay you for that. Yes, you're right. Even if it's not Robin's children, they shouldn't have to go without. What do we do now? I mean, I'm guessing we don't just go up to her and tell her who we are." Cass said that was exactly what they were going to do. "Oh. I guess I figured you'd be a bit on the squeamish side. That's not true. I'm a lot on the squeamish side of doing this. I don't know what I'd even say to her about all this."

"You tell her the truth. That you have only just found out about her. However, I'd start by telling her that Robin is in prison and that he won't be getting out. From the stories I've heard about Robin, it might well be the reason she's living here and not closer to anyone she knows." Robby also knew the sadistic things Robin had done to women. Things he'd also done to men that, in Robby's mind, had been horrendous. "Robby, we don't have to do anything but make sure this woman has money to feed her children and pay her bills."

"Where do we go from here, Cass? I'm not going to have done all this only to sit by and wonder if they might need me. As I said before, this is the only hope I have right now that makes me feel as if I've not been a complete failure as a father and a man."

Cass told him he wasn't even close to being a failure at anything. "Perhaps not now, but I worry. Robin might well have had something wrong with him all along. I don't know. But I do know this family might need me, and I want to help them."

"I understand." He handed him the paperwork he'd gotten at the school board. "This isn't much, but it's the best I could do until we get the rest of the information back. And talk to the mother. She'll be able to give us everything you want if she wishes. Otherwise, I'd advise you to help from a distance. We don't want to piss her off and have her bring charges against you for being a stalker or something along those lines."

The pictures he'd been able to collect showed two little boys, aged nine, playing in the yard. There were also infant pictures of them, as well as a couple of school pictures Cass had been able to unearth. Robby was staring at the two little boys lying in a crib at what he assumed was a hospital.

"I don't remember Robin being this tiny. I'm sure he was at some point, but all my head can think about is that he's an adult. I bet your momma can remember how much each of you weighed when you were born and the exact time." Cass didn't answer him. Not that he required an answer, but he just kept to himself that she most assuredly did know those facts. "Let's go and see this young woman, Cass.

Make an appointment or whatever we need to do. I'll abide by what she tells me. Even if my heart tells me something different."

It took him over three hours to get a phone number for Sarah Linton. She did indeed sleep during the day, according to one of the places that came up on her information. It was, he said, "damned difficult" to call her in early when they needed her.

She worked nearly thirty hours a week at two different restaurants as a waitress and another twenty-five at a place where she sold timeshares. According to that boss, she was a good person to work with, but she was exhausted all the time. He said it made her less friendly to the people there wanting to date her. Neither place seemed to know she had children. Nor did they know where she lived. A post office box number was all they had.

The lady that lived in the apartment below her had two children as well. They would, when necessary, trade-off sitting each other's kids, so they didn't have to pay a sitter. The third job was for her kids to go to a private school. Sarah graded papers for the local teachers at the school where her boys went to pay for extras. Like their lunches. Tuition was paid by her cleaning the place on weekends, with her boys helping. Cass hurt for the way she was struggling to make ends meet.

Once he had the phone number, he was able to

leave a message for her. All he said was his name and that he had some information she needed concerning Robin Quarter. Also, he made sure he told her Robin was in prison. Either she'd call him back or she'd not — it was up to her now. Almost as soon as he closed the connection to his phone, his cell rang back that it was her.

"What do you mean calling me at my home about Robin Quarter? What business is it of yours that —? You said he was in prison. You're sure about that? Last time I heard, he was above such laws and did whatever the fuck he pleased." He heard one of the boys telling her to put a penny in the jar. Cass listened as she told the child she was sorry, then he heard a door closing, shutting off the sounds of the household. "Why are you calling me? Has he told you what he did to me? Do you think to get something from me? I'll tell you right now, I don't have anything, thanks to him. I don't get to see my parents. My sisters and brothers. I lost my job." She sobbed, and he wanted to go there now and take her into his arms. "What is it you want, Mr. Foster? The only thing in the world I have is my sons, and I'd rather die than to let that bastard near them."

"Are they Robin's children?" She said they were. "What do you know of Robin's father? Mr. Robby Quarter."

"I thought he was dead. That's what that prick

told me. That he owned his family ranch and that I should feel privileged that— Why is it I'm telling you this? Do you have some kind of mystical powers? Are you a shifter? That's it, you're making me tell you this personal stuff."

"I am a shifter, Miss Linton. A lion, as a matter of fact. However, I'm not making you tell me. I think you've been through enough without having someone make you relive it. No, I'm not making you. But I will tell you that I have the same strange feelings toward you. That I need to protect and take care of you. I'm sorry about all this, all the things that have happened to you, but Mr. Quarter, Robby, would like to meet you. And the boys. He's only just found out about you three." She asked him why she should believe him. "You shouldn't, I suppose, believe me or him. But what harm can it do for you to meet with us? If you need proof that Robin is in prison, pull up the paper in his hometown. Read how he was arrested for the murder of several people. That rather than stand trial and more than likely get the death penalty, he decided to tell the state where the bodies were and spend the rest of his life in prison, without the chance of parole."

"I don't have a computer. I don't have enough money to pay the electric bill that is overdue at the moment. I'm sure if you've been looking into our lives, you know a good deal more about me than I do you." He told her he was sorry. Then he told her about the money in the bank. "I'm not even going to tell you that you shouldn't have done that. Bouncing a single check could be a trickle-down disaster for us right now. Look, let me talk to my sons. Tell them what's going on and who it is that wants to meet them. I'm not making any promises. They're leerier of people than I am."

"Thank you for this." She said she'd not done anything as yet. "No, but you've given Mr. Quarter a chance, and that's much more than he had before. You call us back at this number and tell us where we can meet you if you decide you will, and we'll be there."

After hanging up, Cass had to calm himself before he spoke to Robby. He didn't want to sound hopeful and then for her call and tell them she'd decided not to see them. But he had enough information now to do some of the things he and Robby had spoken about before. Putting those things into action took a great deal less time than he thought it would have.

Reaching for the phone to call Robby, it rang. Letting out a long breath, he tried his best to sound upbeat while answering. But as soon as he heard the voice on the other end, his lion nearly took him.

"Are you the attorney that talked to our mom? The one that is a lion?" He told the young man he was. "You'd better get over here right now. The man that comes by to get the rent money is going to hurt her again."

"Call the police." He told him he'd done that. "Good. I'm on my way. You and your brother, hide. Someplace where the man can't get to you."

"Good idea."

The phone was dropped, and he could still hear screaming in the background. Going out the door, he held the phone tightly against his ear as he drove like a madman to the address he'd found while doing some work. He was pulling in just as the police were.

When he heard a gunshot sounding, his lion simply took him. As he was racing to the door, it came open, and the children were there. Pushing them out of the way as gently as he could, he moved into the house, smelling blood as he moved. The man in the kitchen was standing over a woman, and rage rolled over him in a way that made Cass sick to his stomach.

Blacking out for a few moments, as if he'd been hit in the head, Cass woke lying in the grass out back of the house. He was clothed and in his human form, and an officer was standing near him. Sitting up, he saw the man turn to him, asking if he was all right now.

"I don't know. What happened?" He told him he'd dragged him out when more police had shown up. "I'm assuming there was a reason for that? Also, that you pulled me out as my other self."

"Yes, you were a lion. Big fucker too. Pardon

my language, sir. But yes, I pulled you out so they'd not know what was going on. Parker Foster showed up too. I don't mean she came in the door saying howdy doody. She just was there when you were finished taking care of Mr. Crabtree. Mrs. Foster said you were her brother-in-law." He nodded and nearly had to be sick from the movement. "She took care that the body wasn't anything like he was. You killed him. Good thing too. He was ready to kill Miss Linton. I'm aware that I'm not making much sense, but this hasn't been an ordinary domestic house call."

"I'm not sure if it's me or what, but it's like you're talking to me in disjointed sentences." He said it was him. That he was scared out of his mind right now. "If Parker said she'd take care of things, she will. Tell me what happened. All I remember is hearing the gunshot and then nothing after my lion took me."

"My partner and I pulled in the same time as you. I wanted to tell you that telling those boys to hide was a good idea. They were coming out to us when you went into the house." Careful not to nod too much, he said he'd had an abusive father. "Miss Linton was in the kitchen telling her landlord, Mr. Crabtree, that she had the money for the rent. He seemed to think she had other means to pay. Needless to say, she took objection to that."

"I just bet she did. Then what happened? Was he going to make her have sex with him?" The officer nodded and said that had been his plan. "Then I showed up."

"Yes, you did. Took his head right off him. Miss Linton had been shot once in the belly by the time you entered. It wasn't until we entered that I realized we might well be in over our heads. I should have waited, but I called in the extras. Mrs. Foster showed up. Just like that, she just appeared and started telling me and my partner what we had to do. She sure is a bossy thing, isn't she?" He looked around, almost as if he was afraid she might have heard him. "The body was lying there with his head off and blood all over the place when the others showed up. They saw what we were told to say. That Miss Linton had saved herself by stabbing him in the chest. Then they took her off to the hospital. Funny thing, though—she was about healed by the time they got here."

It took him a few moments to realize what he'd said. After he sat there for a little while longer, all his thoughts centered on Sarah. He had a feeling she'd healed because of him. When he was ready to stand up, Parker met him at the doorway to the house. She looked like she was as happy as he was.

"She's going to be just fine. They took her to the hospital right after it was determined it was self-defense. I've called Robby in. He's with the boys now. They're getting to know one another. Are you all right?" He shrugged. "Good. There are several things you should be made aware of. First of all, you weren't here. I'm sure you might have guessed that part, but I just need to put that out there. Second, the house is now a part of the Foster group. We purchased it just today, so we have the rights to do with it as we want. Which will be tearing it down as soon as the police are finished with it. No one needs to be seeing this place and thinking about the death that occurred here. Especially not those young boys. Who I like, by the way."

"I've not met them yet." She nodded and didn't continue. Nor did she seem inclined to tell him anything else. "What are you not telling me? Just tell me, Parker. You look like you have a fart crosswise, and it's paining you."

"You Foster men. I do have something to tell you, but I think you might well be aware of it already. She's your mate. Also, the kids are Robin's. I'm assuming that was why you were coming out here." Cass told her about one of the boys calling him. "They're not speaking. Not to any of us. When asked how the man had gotten into the house, they clammed up tighter than you can be when you're on a case."

"Are you thinking they might have let him in and are feeling badly for it?" She said she knew that was what had happened. "Are they hurt? Where is Sarah? I know you said she was taken to the hospital, but the young cop told me she'd started to heal. I'm guessing either you did something to her, or it was me being her mate."

"You. The kids were hurt, but not terribly. That is what I've been working up to. He's been bullying them all along. Making them let him in the house when she's not at home. Or worse yet, when she's sleeping. I've heard of this happening before, but this guy would take pictures of her sleeping. The boys are sick with it, the worry that they caused their mother to nearly die. Which she did, by the way. They need to be sat down and told what the hell is going on. Also, they weren't the least bit afraid of you showing up as a big badassed lion. I guess their mother told them what you were."

"Yes. I'm assuming so too. The one that called me, he knew what I was. When I told him to hide with his brother, he just dropped the phone and bugged the hell out. I wonder how they knew to call me." Parker said his phone number was by the phone when she'd gotten there. That Sarah must have written it down. "And they were supposed to talk about us coming to meet them."

"Sounds about right." She asked him where he was going now. "I'm guessing the hospital. If so, I'd like to ride along. I want to check on the boys as well as Sarah. You'll have to talk to her soon, and I would like to be there in the event she has any questions about the magic I can only assume she got."

"Why? I mean, other than mine, you're assuming she got something from you as well?" Parker nodded but didn't look very happy. "What happened, Parker? Am I going to be afraid of her when I go see her? To be honest with you, I've only ever seen a picture of her and the boys. Not to mention the one of her was slightly blurry, and the boys were just school pictures. Those never show what a child really looks like."

They spoke all the way to the hospital. By the time they arrived, he was ready to go back to the house and wait. Nothing, he thought, could have prepared him for the shit Parker knew about his mate and children. Nothing that would have been on paper anyway.

"She had this good life—a wonderfully supportive family—and Robin took it all away by taking her from her date, who he killed, then raping her. The fucker then shot her three times in the chest and left her for dead. If not for the police being called when they were and them knowing about the death of Dennis, her then boyfriend, it might well have been too late for her." Cass listened to Parker, but his mind was centered on the fact that she might well have died twice before he would have met her. "As it turned out, Robin found out that she was alive and tormented her for the next several months. When she found out she was going to have his child, they faked her suicide, and she moved out here to raise them on their own. I'm going to have someone notify her family that she's safe now, as soon as we can get her and the boys together."

He was as ready as he'd ever been, he supposed when he knocked on the door to her room. Even as he opened it, he could hear crying. The children were on the bed with her, and Robby was sitting in the chair. All four of them looked like they'd been talking and crying for some time now.

~*~

Quin watched his brother tangle with the pretty little blonde. She wasn't like the other women in the family. She was outspoken, but it was tempered with her pain. The little boys, Toby and Mike, seemed to be watching them too. They looked like they were watching a tennis match with their blond heads going back and forth between the two of them.

"How about we go get some lunch?" The boys, who he was talking to, nearly leapt at him when he spoke. "I think we can do better than hospital food. How would some pizza or burgers sound? Or better yet, we can hit some of the kinds of places that cater to people with a larger range of tastes." They both looked at him oddly. "Or not. What do you want?"

"Are you going to be our uncle?" Quin hadn't thought of it but told them he was. "Okay, you might want to remember that we're only kids. We don't have a range of tastes. Just burgers is good. We had pizza last week, and neither of us liked it all that much."

"Really? What did it have on it?" Toby, the one that seemed to do most of the talking, said it was from their school and had strips of something *like* pepperoni, but he was positive it wasn't. "I've had school pizza before. You're right. It's only *like* pepperoni."

They were waiting at the elevator when Robby asked to join them. Both of the kids had taken his hand when they'd left the room, but Mike took Robby's hand as they entered the elevator. Going out of the hospital was refreshing. The air inside smelled of things he didn't care to think about.

"Do you have any kids we can play with? Mom is so busy all the time we don't get to play with the kids at school. Not that we like them. They're very snobby." Mike agreed with Toby, saying they had chips on their shoulders. "Not chips, you dummy. A chip on their shoulder. Will you pay attention when you hear someone using those things?"

"For a long time I thought it was chips too. I was forever looking for the chips. But as I grew older, I realized it was only a chip, and I never cared for that saying." Mike asked Robby why. "Well, it labels people. I try hard not to do that when I meet someone. I mean, just because they're dressed nice or have a big smile on their faces, it doesn't mean they're rich or happy. Take this man here, for example. What is it you think Quin does for a living? Unless he's told you."

"He smells good. And he's a nice man. I feel good when I'm around him. Not like I did when Mr. Crabtree came around." Toby poked his brother. "Oh. I forgot."

"It's all right if you talk about the man. And the things he did when your mom wasn't around. Now there is another example of a person that didn't look like what he was." Mike said he was a pervert. "Yes, he was. A mean one on top of that. But when a person would see him out on the street, they'd think to themselves, 'There goes Mr. Crabtree. He rents houses to people.' But what they should have been thinking was, 'There goes that mean man who takes advantage of young boys trying to protect their mother.' Like you two."

Mike nodded, but Toby looked up at him. "You look like you don't work much. I know you do. You have on a nice shirt and pants, and your shoes look new." Quin told him they were indeed new, as he'd stepped in horse manure the other morning, and his wife wouldn't allow him to wear them in the house anymore. "Were you looking to step in horse poop?"

"No. I'm a vet. I take care of Mr. Quarter's horses for him when they need it. Also, I check out their newborns when they come along and go with him when there is a horse race that his ponies are in." They both looked at Robby like he was a god then. "You should ask your mom if you could go to a couple of races with your new grandda. They're fun. My niece goes too. You'll like all the other kids in the family. My oldest brother has twin little girls. They're beautiful."

"But you don't have any kids." Quin told Mike he didn't yet. "Yet. Okay. Who is your wife, and why isn't she here? Everybody else is, it seems."

"They're not. Trust me, I have a large family. I have five brothers, now three sisters-in-law, my mom, and my grandma. I also am happy to say I have a wonderful set of in-laws that I love. My mom will be so happy to be hanging around with you guys. You'll have all the fresh baked cookies you can eat. Then there are the kids." Smiling, he named off all the children in the family. "My mom owns this barn. I know that sounds like nothing, but it's huge. It has room in it to have large parties and weddings. But the best part is when I was leaving to come out here, there was playground equipment being put in. Swings, slides. I think there was some kind of climbing equipment. I didn't get to see it all, but I was told that kids from everywhere would want to use it. And you guys will be able to whenever your mom lets you because your grandma owns it all."

"Wow."

They both asked if they could have chocolate milk with their dinner, and while he figured it would be all right, he asked his brother. Without a connection to Sarah yet, he had to rely on him doing the asking for him.

She said they can have one chocolate or two white. Up to them. They're not allergic to anything either. He said that was going to be his next question before they ordered. *Sarah said to tell them that ketchup is not a veggie, nor are French fries. They have to offset their meal with something green.*

He told the boys what their mother had said. The look of disappointment on their faces made him laugh. Quin told Cass.

Sarah said they don't get out much, so be gentle with them when they don't have any idea what to order. Where are you? He told him. After a few minutes, Cass was laughing. *Sarah wants to know if she orders two milks. Can you bring her back a pizza too? She wants a meat one with all the trimmings. I'm not sure what that means, but you might be able to guess. We're doing better now that we're alone.*

Good. I'm having a blast myself.

When he ordered the pizzas, he also put in an order for one to go. The waiter told them he'd not put in the order until they were about finished. As soon as their meal was put in front of them, the boys looked at each other then back at their meal. "Is there something wrong with it? You said you'd like to try one like your mom liked."

"It's nothing like the ones they serve at our school." Toby nodded as he got help from Robby on how to pick it up. It was hotter, too, apparently. "Holy smokes, Uncle Quin, this is the best thing I've ever eaten. This is amazing."

They not only ate their personal-sized pizza but a part of his and Robby's. It was fun to watch them enjoying themselves so much, and he was glad they were enjoying the food. He figured that the green peppers on the pizza, though they had picked most of them off, was their green veggie, and not a bit of ketchup was poured onto anything.

When are you coming back? He asked his brother if he missed him. *No. But she's missing the kids. I think she only just realized they weren't with anyone she knew. I swore to her they were in the safest hands in the world. But seriously, I hope you bring back enough pizza for me to have some too. I'm starving.*

He ordered two more pizzas to go and told his brother they were just getting finished up and would be there in about twenty minutes. It was nearly that time when they entered the room with the pizzas and a gallon of white milk. Cass liked milk with his pie as well.

"I hope you don't mind, but I'm having food delivered to the staff here." Sarah looked surprised but didn't comment. "They do a great job, and I wanted to make sure they knew we appreciate them taking such good care of everyone. The other two shifts will have some as well."

It was nearly midnight, and the boys had been dozing in the chairs when he made his way back to the hotel he was staying in. Mike and Toby came with him after promises of making sure they brushed their teeth and took a bath. He didn't know if the hotel room had a bathtub, but Sarah said a shower would be just as good. Quin and Robby ordered things online to have delivered to the hotel for in the morning, and they were set. Lucky for them, the kids still had tags on their clothing that they could know the sizes from.

Just as he was going to bed, he heard from Rogue. *I really am pissed off about this shit. I want to meet them too.* He'd just told her what they'd done tonight with them and how much he loved hanging around with them. Robby also seemed to be a lot less tense. *I have it on good authority that Robin isn't playing well with the other inmates. Today he got into a fight and had to get stitches. He keeps this up, and he's going to be dead before long.*

I don't think Robby cares one way or the other now that he has a family around him. He and Sarah seem to be hitting it off well. I really had to restrain him from buying out the store when he and I ordered things they'll need for the next few days. I think tomorrow we're headed to the zoo.

I've not been to the zoo in ages. I would guess that lions have a good deal of respect for you guys when you show up. He laughed. *Anyway, I'm nearly finished here, and if I can, I'm going to see about getting dropped off there. That way I can have some fun with them too. By the way, Brook has started on the house for my dad and Lexi. There are two homes near one another that she's hoping Sarah and the boys will want to stay in. At least until she and Cass get things worked out. Then we can rent it out. But I was thinking he'd like them on the ranch. Either way is good for us. So long as we can help her out when she needs it. Do you think she'll need it?*

She really wants to see her family, Cass told me. I guess she's not been able to see them since the boys were born. That's sad if you ask me. Rogue said she could understand that. *Why don't you see what you can find out about them before they're notified? They might be the worst kind of people, and she doesn't want to be around them.*

I'll get on that. She laughed and told him she wanted children. *As soon as possible. I mean, it's not like we'd not have an abundance of sitters. Even if you don't count the aunts and uncles and grandparents, there are enough kids around that would jump at the chance of sitting for us and the others.*

After telling her he loved her, she told him she loved him as well. Children would be wonderful, he thought and told her that as well. He was thinking he'd like to have a houseful but knew it wasn't up to him. It was her body, and he had no doubt Rogue would tell him when she'd had enough. Smiling, he rolled over and closed his eyes. Quin was looking forward to tomorrow.

Chapter 9

Hanging up the phone, Tommy had a few minutes to himself as he stood there thinking of what he'd just been told. Robin Quarter was in jail, and his little girl had met someone. Not that he didn't believe his little girl could care for herself, but he liked that Ms. Foster had filled him in on Cassidy Foster and what sort of means he had to take care of the three of them.

"Tommy, what is it? You sounded upset." He told his wife of nearly fifty years what the call had been about. Michell sat down on the chair. He was glad there had been one there for her to use. "Is she coming home?"

"She's in the hospital. I was told it's nothing more than a precaution. The landlord she was renting from, he tried to hurt her." He didn't say more. Michell seemed to understand. "We were asked to decide what we want to do about seeing her. And the boys. Like that would ever be something we'd have to think about."

"Who called you?" He had to glance at his notes, knowing he had to get the name right the first time or he'd not remember it. "An FBI agent? In the family? My goodness. Whatever are we to think about that?"

"Nothing. The man that is Sarah's mate—she did say, mate—is an attorney. A good one, too, apparently. He works for the family. And even had she not told me, I know who the Fosters are." She said she had heard of them as well. Tommy sat down. "Do we tell the others or wait until we know things? I haven't any idea what that might be, but you tell me, and I'll call them. Jude will be thrilled beyond words. He's missed his sister."

Jude didn't know who his sister was, but he thought saying it like he had made his wife feel better. Jude had been born with the cord wrapped tightly around his little throat and had suffered brain damage. He was a good boy at thirty-six, and perhaps he did miss Sarah, but not as his sister, Tommy thought. Just someone he'd not seen in a long time.

"We'll have a hotel room set up for us, she told me. Also that if the others were wanting to come, they'd send their plane for us." He had to laugh a little. "Their plane. I don't know if I've even been on a domestic flight, much less a private one."

"Yes, you have. Our honeymoon." He was joking but again kept it to himself. This was serious business here, and he didn't want his wife upset. "Should we call the others?"

"Yes. If we don't tell them, they'll be upset. Not that they'll be upset for long, but it might be nice to have them with us when we meet her new family." He thought of the boys and the pictures he had of them that were almost as old as they were now. "They'd be nine about now. I've only seen them the one time, and that wasn't nearly enough. Grandsons. I need to see them as much as I do our Sarah."

"Me as well, Tommy. I've so missed her." She stood up, then sat again. "I just want to think about this for a moment longer. The thought of seeing them all, it's just like a dream, and I don't think I ever want to wake from it. Are you sure that man is in prison? He should have gone long ago, but we just didn't have the money to sue him. And Sarah wouldn't hear of it. Oh, Tommy, I want to have a hug from them so desperately. Did this woman say when we could go?"

"Today if we've got a mind to." He wanted to leave right that moment, but he knew there were things to be planned and such. "She told me that Robby Quarter is there with her. That he'd only just found out about Sarah and the boys. I don't know why, but I had it in my head that we were told he was dead."

"Yes, we were told that. But then every other thing coming out of the monster's mouth has been nothing but bologna. It's a small wonder he's been put away. Did she tell you how he was caught?" Tommy said he'd not thought to ask. "Well, I suppose we can get to that when we get there. I'll call the girls, you call Michael. Tell them…. I guess we should plan on this trip for the morning if they're really going to send something to go in. It certainly will be much cheaper this way."

"I agree."

He didn't tell her they'd offered to pay for them to be in a hotel if they were all to come. Remembering to do that so she could tell Shelly and April so they'd not be out anything but a couple of days work, he called his son. Michael was about as thrilled as he'd been when he'd heard they could see Sarah.

"I'd have to see about money, Dad. As much as I'd love to go and give her a hug, I can't afford much right now." He told him what the Fosters had said. "For all of us? I mean, my wife and child too? Dad, Sarah hasn't met Belinda or my son yet. We were married after she left home to hide out. I'd love to be able to take them too. You see, and if that can be done, I'm all in for it. I'll be there whenever they tell us to be."

After finding out his daughters had said the same thing about having things paid for, he was happy to know they were willing to drop everything to go see their sister. He'd not thought of how she might not have seen some of the kids yet, and that made him cry just a little. Sarah had missed so much. They'd missed so much too.

He made a head count and was sure they'd tell him it was just too many people. Fourteen of them converging on a generous family was a lot to deal with. Not to mention hotel accommodations. So when he called Mrs. Foster back, Tommy was prepared for her to tell him just that. However, she was excited that Sarah would see her entire family and didn't say a word about how many.

"You tell me how many per room, Mr. Linton, and I'll work that into the hotel. Also, we've rented out a restaurant that was being fixed up to feed us all tomorrow night." He couldn't believe people were being this nice to his family and told her that. "You're going to be our family as well, and we make sure family is all taken care of. You'll get to meet all of Cass's family too. I did tell you they were lions, correct? So don't be surprised if they're a little larger than normal men."

"My daughter-in-law, Belinda, is a lion. We know a few other shifters as well." Parker, as she told him to call her, was happy to hear that. "Parker, this is going to be expensive. I mean, I've heard about your family, and I still think this is a great deal of money to be putting out for a family you don't know."

"No, it's not. We'd pay more just to have Sarah happy. I think she's a little down with all this going on. By the way, she has no idea you're all coming. We thought it would be a lovely surprise for her and the boys to see you all." He said it certainly would. Then he told her about the nieces and nephews she'd not met. "Then it will be twice as wonderful for her. Tommy, you leave the arrangements to me, and we'll have a party like no one has ever seen before."

"I'm sure of that." He laughed when she did. "All right. If you can make the arrangements for us to come there tomorrow, we'll be at the airport. There are a lot of us, so we might have to make a couple of trips to give me some time."

"I'm sending limos to get you all." He nearly sobbed when she told him it was part of their welcome to the family plan. "It would be wonderful if you could make sure everyone is meeting up at your home. It will save us some time to get you out here."

He called his family back and told them what was going on. All of them were going to come home tonight and be there in the morning. Since he knew it would take them a while to get packed and such, he told them they'd have dinner here, and that should give them plenty of time. Glancing at his clock, he thought that in eight hours, his kids, for the most part, would be all under one roof for the first time in ages.

Bedtime came later than he wanted, but it was wonderful to see his kids. Jude had to be taken outside a couple of times — it got to be too much for him. But he loved the kids, and he played with them as much as they did each other. He could only imagine what the Fosters would make of him when he was upset.

At eight sharp, the limos pulled into their drive. The neighbors were out looking at the sight as he started loading up suitcases into the vans. He didn't care. Tommy was going to see his little girl, and they could fly a fig for all he cared.

Once the men had the vans loaded up, they went ahead to the airport to start on the trip. Car seats had been provided, which he thought was very nice, as well as snacks for the kids to munch on. There were even some things for Jude, which he thought was well beyond a nice thing anyone could have done for them.

Loading into the plane took less time than he thought it should have, and a few minutes after he was seated and buckled in, they were in the air. Christ, he thought, looking around at his family. This was all possible because of the kindness of strangers.

A man came back to speak to them just as the seatbelt sign was turned off. "Hello, everyone. My name is Cassidy Foster. Everyone calls me Cass. Sarah is my mate." The applause had the younger man's face turning a bright pink. "I came along to answer any questions I could about not just Sarah and her being hurt, but anything else I can do for you. But in the meantime, I've brought you a little surprise."

The boys came out of the cockpit, and Tommy nearly knocked his wife out of the way to get to them. My goodness, Tommy thought, they were handsome little men. All of them hugged them, telling them how excited they were to come along, and by the time they were landing in the little airport near a city called Zanesville, Toby was sitting on his lap, and Mike was sitting with his grandma.

"You've given us a great gift, young man. Not just in having the boys here, but with bringing us to my daughter." Cass said it was his pleasure, but he'd wanted to meet them as well. "Yes, well, you might want to take that back when we all converge on my daughter's room and drive you insane."

"Mr. Linton, I have a very large family myself. I know loud. But Sarah is at the hotel now. They released her this morning, and my brother made sure she was taken there for us to have more room. My sister-in-law, Rogue, has a Ph.D. in forensic photography, but she is also a good doctor. She's making sure she doesn't overdo it before we arrive." He was impressed at the jobs they all had. "You weren't told this, and I'm sure you'll find out anyway, but Parker, you've spoken to her, she's a witch. An honest to goodness witch. We're all sorts of things when you get right down to it."

There was a lot to think about, but he pushed it

all to the back of his mind. The ride to the hotel seemed to take forever, but it was made easier with Toby and Mike with them. The boys told them all about their life. He was sure there was worse than they were saying, but they were happy, and to Tommy, that was more than enough.

Pulling into the parking lot of not a cheap hotel as he had thought, but a very nice one, Tommy suddenly had second thoughts. He wasn't sure she'd welcome them. That Sarah had somehow changed. But when Toby pulled him free of the first luxury he'd had in forever, Tommy went into the hotel. There his Sarah was talking to Cass, who had left ahead of them.

"Daddy? Mom?"

That was all it took for him to lose it. Sarah hugged them all, marveling over the babies and her family. Even Jude was excited and hugged Sarah several times, as they all did. It was a homecoming he was glad the Fosters had made possible for them all.

Before You Go...

HELP AN AUTHOR

write a review

THANK YOU!

Share your voice and help guide other readers to these wonderful books. Even if it's only a line or two, your reviews help readers discover the author's books so they can continue creating stories that you'll love. Log in to your favorite retailer and leave a review. Thank you.

AWARD WINNING, BESTSELLING AUTHOR

Kathi Barton, a winner of the Pinnacle Book Achievement award as well as a best-selling author on Amazon and All Romance books, lives in Nashport, Ohio, with her husband, Paul. When not creating new worlds and romance, Kathi and her husband enjoy camping and going to auctions. She can also be seen at county fairs with her husband, who is an artist and potter.

Her muse, a cross between Jimmy Stewart and Hugh Jackman, brings her stories to life for her readers in a way that has them coming back time and again for more. Her favorite genre is paranormal romance, with a great deal of spice. You can visit Kathi on line and drop her an email if you'd like. She loves hearing from her fans. aaronskiss@gmail.com.

Follow Kathi on her blog: http://kathisbartonauthor.blogspot.com/

www.ingramcontent.com/pod-product-compliance
Lightning Source LLC
Chambersburg PA
CBHW030225180626
46810CB00008B/2974